BOOK ONE: DYSPHORIA

BLACK SWAN

MARK GOODWIN

Technical information in the book is included to convey realism. The author shall not have liability or responsibility to any person or entity with respect to any loss or damage caused, or allegedly caused, directly or indirectly by the information contained in this book.

All of the characters, places, and incidents are products of the author's imagination or are used fictitiously. Any resemblance to actual people, places, or events is entirely coincidental.

Copyright © 2019 Goodwin America Corp.

All rights reserved. No part of this publication may be reproduced, stored in a retrieval system, or transmitted in any form or by any means without the prior written permission of the author, except by a reviewer who may quote short passages in a review.

ISBN: 9781072671039

ACKNOWLEDGMENTS

I would like to thank my Editor in Chief Catherine Goodwin, as well as the rest of my fantastic editing team, Jeff Markland, Frank Shackleford, Stacey Glemboski, Sherrill Hesler, and Claudine Allison.

A special thanks to Captain Manny Bande NYPD ESU Retired for consultation on all things tactical and police procedural.

I'd also like to say thank you to Dan Hesler for medical advice.

PROLOGUE

Thy silver is become dross, thy wine mixed with water.

Isaiah1:22

US economic policy of late has been all about political posturing and nothing about long-term sustainability. But, to be fair to our noble politicians on both sides of the aisle, the ship of long-term sustainability sailed long ago.

Economists refer to the rare events that trigger financial chaos as black swans. Swans are usually white, and seeing a black swan is less common. Nevertheless, black swans exist and perhaps in greater quantities than the economists' analogy would lead us to believe. It is estimated that the global population of black swans is near 500,000, not quite worthy of the endangered species list. Likewise, catastrophic financial upheaval is a regular occurrence, and the policies that trigger them are the rule more often than the exception.

At the time of this writing, the US Debt is at $23 trillion and the annual deficit is $1 trillion. Politicians who dare to address the matter are quickly labeled as pariahs by their respective parties and shuffled to a dark corner of the room. This is a debt that can never be repaid. The best our elected leaders can hope for is to devalue the debt by abasing the currency our debt is denominated in, the US Dollar.

All the king's horses and all the king's men have no better alternative than to destroy the very medium of exchange and store of value that our society is founded upon. It is the tool the Romans resorted to in order to maintain a burgeoning welfare state and finance a global military presence. It became the last-ditch effort of the Weimar Republic to escape their war and reparation debts after World War I. Russia pursued a similar policy in the 90s, Argentina in 2001, Zimbabwe in 2008, and most recently, Venezuela.

Students of history can tell you that in none of those cases did the experiment end well. So why do governments do it? Quite literally, they have no other choice.

The reality of US debt is even worse. Twenty-three trillion is only the tip of the iceberg. Once we add in unfunded liabilities, which consist of things like Social Security, federal pensions, and Medicare, to the tune of an additional $210 trillion, you quickly realize that the coming crisis is baked into the cake. We've passed the point of no return. Like a locomotive barreling at full speed down the track toward a missing bridge, when it comes, the impact will be brutal. Or, to return to the ship and iceberg analogies, the Titanic has already scraped the jagged edges, her hull is ripped open like an aluminum foil swan from a Chinese restaurant, and she's taking on water fast. Soon, our entire economy will be rolling over into the icy waters of the abyss.

In all of the instances listed previously, cataclysmic periods of mass starvation, violence, and rioting ensued. It would be beyond naive to imagine that the end of the US Dollar should be any different. If you have the slightest inclination toward self-preservation, now would be a magnificent time to begin making your way to the lifeboats.

CHAPTER 1

The earth also was corrupt before God, and the earth was filled with violence.

Genesis 6:11

Stepping out onto New York City's West 44th Street, Country music guitar legend Shane Black smelled the noxious odor of burning rubber. The year was off to a bad start. Instead of noisemakers and fireworks, the sounds of dissent and remonstration pierced the air in the first minutes of January 1st. "We've got about 14 blocks to get back to the hotel. Don't stop for anything. Manhattan is coming unglued." Holding his fiancé's hand, Shane led his small entourage up 6th Ave.

"Where's my bailout? Where's my future?" The monotonous chant of the rioters in Times Square grew fainter with each block Shane's group passed. Yet the audible void left by the angst-filled mantra was quickly replaced by the noise of looting and vandalism.

Shane watched hooligans smash out several first-floor windows of Rockefeller Center as his group hurried past.

Head of security Bobby Grant did his best to keep himself between the group and any potential threats. "Let's try moving a little faster."

Pointing at the flaming vehicle in front of them Shane's fiancé, Lilith, said with a panicked voice, "That bus is on fire!"

"I'm sure no one was inside when they lit it up." Derrick Collum held his wife's hand and kept walking at a steady clip.

More ruffians smashed against the box office windows of Radio City Music Hall with tire irons and baseball bats.

Shortly after they passed 53rd Street, a young man brushed up against Shane. "Hey bro! They just broke into the currency exchange! Come on, we might get some foreign cash that will actually buy something!"

Shane held up a hand and kept walking. "Thanks, but I'm good."

With his free hand, the young man pulled down his bandana to reveal his expression of mock surprise. "You're good? What? You don't need any more money?" The looter yelled to his colleagues, "Hey guys, I think we just found some one-percenters." He waved for his comrades to join him while his other hand held a length of metal pipe.

Several of the thugs who were obviously in his crew stopped what they were doing and began to circle around Shane's group. All held various items which could be used as weapons.

Completely unarmed, Shane eyed the collection of tire irons, baseball bats, and pieces of metal pipe. He put himself between Lilith and the thugs, wondering how they'd ever get out of this situation alive.

***

Nine Days Earlier, December 23

Shane glanced over at Lilith then turned his attention back to the highway. Two lines on the otherwise-white-powdered pavement showed the path of the travelers who'd gone before them. The flakes grew larger and even from the elevated cab of the 4x4 GMC Sierra Denali, visibility was deteriorating fast. "I told you that you didn't have to come."

"Relax!" she exclaimed. "I know what I'm getting myself into. I've met plenty of people like your parents. Trust me, my good-girl act is pretty convincing. I even brought church clothes for Christmas Eve service.

"Tell me, what's the church like? Is it a little white church with stained glass and a steeple, like on a Christmas card?"

He sighed. "Not exactly. The church finally got its own building. It used to be an Ingles grocery store. When Publix finally came to the area, they pushed grocers with high prices and poor selections out of the market."

"A grocery store? You're kidding me!" She slapped his leg.

"No. Before that, they were renting space in a school."

"No way. Like your parents think they're too good for a regular church?"

Shane laughed at her interpretation of the facts. "Not too good, but they see things differently than most churches around town. Don't judge them before you've met them. They're really nice folks."

She crossed her arms. "And I suppose you've asked them not to judge me, right?"

"They're not like that. They'll love on you, even if they don't approve of our . . . living arrangement."

"Mmhmm. I'm the harlot who seduced their perfect little boy into living in sin."

Shane watched the flurries melting against the windshield. "I just hope we don't get snowed in. Three days of sleeping in separate rooms is about all I can handle."

"Maybe I'll sneak into your room." She bit her red-polished fingernail and put on her bedroom eyes.

He shook his head adamantly. "Oh, no! Don't even think about it. My mom will know."

"Are you still scared of your mommy? You're thirty-five years old and the lead guitarist for the biggest country band in America. Which, by the way, most parents would die to have a son as successful as you."

"I'm not afraid of them, but I respect their rules when I'm in their house."

"Whatever." Lilith flipped her long blonde hair over her shoulder and began pecking at the screen of her phone with her nails. "Getting snowed in isn't an option anyway. We have to be in Times Square for New Year's Eve. You guys are the only country music headliners this year. I had to pull a lot of strings and issue some IOUs to get Backwoods on the ticket. It's not like we can just reschedule for next year."

Lilith glanced up from her phone. "You never told me why a prominent CPA like your father would sell his practice in Charlotte and move to some little hick town in the North Carolina mountains. What did you say the name of this place is?"

"Sylva. It's a long story."

"It's a long trip from Nashville to the middle of nowhere. I've got time."

Shane took a deep breath and considered how to relay the information to Lilith without making his parents sound like lunatics. "Do you remember the Y2K bug, the computer glitch that was supposed to cause all the disruptions in the year 2000?"

"I was six, so no, I don't remember much about that year."

"Well, my dad was convinced the wheels were going to come off. Most people who understood the problem say we narrowly missed a catastrophic event. My dad wanted a place where we could be safe and take care of ourselves. Grow our own food, that sort of thing."

"I don't understand. The year 2000 was a long time ago. Why did he keep your family out in the middle of the sticks for the next two decades?"

"They liked the lifestyle. And according to my dad, Y2K was only the beginning of the systemic threats."

"Watch out!" Lilith screamed.

Shane took his foot off of the gas and fought his natural inclination to slam on the brakes. He steered away from the car in front of him, which had hit a patch of ice. The car spun out of control. The vehicle seemed to be regaining control, but suddenly fishtailed into Shane's pickup, then slid off the shoulder and down the embankment.

Shane slowly pulled to the side of the road. He looked at Lilith. "Are you alright?"

"Frightened is all." Lilith shot a look of disdain at the vehicle in the ditch. "People shouldn't be driving their little Walmart cars around in this kind of weather."

"Walmart cars?"

"Yeah." She waved her hand at the older-model Pontiac Sunbird with faded paint. "These things litter the parking lots of Walmarts all over the country, not that I'd go to Walmart anyway."

"I'm going to see if they're okay." Shane opened his door.

"Get their insurance info, if they even have any. The front quarter panel of your truck is a mess."

Shane closed the door and walked carefully in the snow. Cowboy boots offered little in the traction department.

The late-twenties woman in the driver's seat

rolled down her window. "I'm so sorry about your truck!"

Shane leaned on the top of the car and glanced back at the mangled fender of his Sierra. "It's just a scratch. Are you folks okay?"

The woman looked at the little girl in the passenger's seat and the toddler boy in the back car seat. "We're fine."

Shane saw no ring on the woman's finger and figured she was raising the two kids on her own. "I wish I had a tow strap. I'd pull you out."

"I'll call a tow truck. And I suppose we should call the police, right?"

Shane guessed the woman could ill afford a tow truck or an increase in insurance premiums due to a wreck. "I don't see a need for all of that."

"But your truck, my insurance will pay for it."

"Like I said, it's just a scratch. It'll probably buff out. And let me call a tow truck for you." Shane took out his phone to search for a tow company.

"Mama, you know who that is, don't you?" The little girl looked to be nine or ten years old.

"No, honey." The woman looked closer at Shane.

"It's Shane Black, from Backwoods. Can we take your picture?"

Shane smiled. "Let me finish this call, and we'll get a couple of selfies together."

The little girl rushed out of the car with her mother's phone. She waited patiently for Shane to give his credit card information to the tow company. Once he completed the call, she said with exuberance, "My friends at school are never going to believe this. I write my own songs, you know.

Mama's going to get me a guitar for Christmas, and I'm going to move to Nashville when I get older."

The mother's face looked tired. "I said I'd get you a guitar sometime. It might not be this year, baby. Things are tight."

"That's fine. I'll have more songs written by next Christmas anyway." The little girl smiled and snapped several pictures with Shane. "I have this month's Country Music People magazine with Backwoods on the cover. Will you sign it for me?"

Shane thrilled at the spirited young girl who refused to be daunted by her circumstances. "Sure, baby. I think I might have a Sharpie in the truck."

Shane returned to his vehicle and opened the back door. "Can you pass me the marker in the console?"

Lilith handed him the Sharpie. "Why are you getting out your guitar? You gonna play Jingle Bells on the side of the road?"

"No. I'm gonna give it to that little girl."

"You're going to give her a $5,000.00 custom guitar? Does she even know how to play?"

"She'll learn." He closed the door and brought the case to the girl. "Merry Christmas."

The little girl seemed to stop breathing for a moment. She looked at her mother as if asking for permission.

The mother's eyes welled up with tears first, then the little girl's did likewise.

Shane hugged her close and recommended YouTube for getting started with the basics.

***

Forty minutes later, the tow truck pulled the mother's car free from snow. Shane waved as he pulled away. "Y'all be safe. Merry Christmas." He rolled up the window and continued the trip home.

"I can't believe we had to wait for the tow truck!" Lilith protested. "You know, you're really good at being a star, it's just that you do it at all the wrong times, when it doesn't matter."

"What do you mean?"

"Like this right here, if we'd had a camera rolling, that would have been great PR. But sometimes it's like you're allergic to success."

"Backwoods has won four Country Music Awards in five years. How do you figure?"

"Like this CMT interview when we get back from New York. Why is it just Derrick? You were invited to participate, but you turned it down."

"Derrick is the front man. He gets paid more than the rest of us. It's part of his job to be the public face."

"I appreciate that you're a nice guy, Shane, but you're also very naive. The way things are going, Derrick Collum could go on tour tomorrow, and no one would ever bat an eye at it not being Backwoods."

"Derrick would never do that to us."

"If Bridgett starts pushing him in that direction, who do you think he'll choose to disappoint, his wife-slash-manager or his bandmates?"

"Bridgett is the band's manager, not Derrick's."

"Keep telling yourself that." Lilith reapplied her lipstick.

"Did Bridgett say something to you?"

"No. But if she did, we'd still be friends because Bridgett and I understand the business side of things."

"Why did you have to put this in my head right before Christmas?" Shane grumbled.

"It's reality, hun. Nashville might have a sweet veneer, but just below the surface, it's as cut-throat as any other big city; maybe even more so. The music industry is as mean as it gets. You need to stay on your guard."

Shane didn't want to be keyed up, wondering when he'd be stabbed in the back by his closest friends. And he certainly wanted to hear no more about it from Lilith. He turned on the radio and scrolled through for some traditional Christmas tunes.

Four songs played, then the station cut to a news break.

"Investors aren't getting what they asked for this year on the last trading day before Christmas. Rather than the much-anticipated Santa Clause rally so many analysts have predicted, investors are getting lumps of coal. Trading was halted for fifteen minutes shortly after open this morning when the Dow Jones dropped more than 2000 points and the S&P lost just under 300 points. Since reopening, the bloodletting has continued with the Dow currently sitting at 3,500 points below yesterday's close and the S&P down by 560 points. This puts the markets precariously close to triggering the second circuit breaker for the day, which would suspend trading for another fifteen minutes. From there, if markets drop another seven percent, they'll be closed for the remainder of the day.

"For those of you following the ongoing pension crisis, today's losses so far equate to $5 trillion of wealth that has been erased. Today's losses could be the death knell for states like New Jersey, Illinois, and Kentucky. Even states like California, which had higher funded ratios, may be pushed to the brink by today's bloodletting.

"Massive exoduses from high-tax states like California and New York since the Tax Cuts and Jobs Act have eroded the tax base as high earners fled to more tax-friendly locales. This massive blow to state revenues had many states operating in crisis mode even before this morning's carnage on Wall Street."

Shane turned off the radio. Heavy creases grew in his forehead as he calculated the losses in his own retirement account.

"I told you, you should have invested in my friend's horse breeding farm up in Kentucky." Lilith's thumbs typed away on her phone.

"I don't know anything about horses." Shane knew even less about her friend but didn't add this fact to the conversation.

"You don't know anything about stocks either." Her eyes flicked up, but only for a moment. "Mama horses and daddy horses get together and have baby horses. It's a lot simpler than trying to calculate the forward earnings of Apple, Google, and Facebook."

"Let's just try to enjoy Christmas. Maybe

everyone will go home, have some eggnog and the markets will bounce back on Tuesday." Shane turned off the main road and drove up the long gravel driveway toward his parents' cabin.

"Wishful thinking might not help much, but I suppose it doesn't hurt anything either," Lilith said. "Heaven knows I've done my share of it leading up to coming here."

"Is that it?" Lilith pointed at a modest board-and-batten cabin with a timber frame porch.

"No." Shane nodded toward the large rough-hewn cabin at the top of the hill in front of them. "It's that one."

"Who lives in the little one?"

"My dad runs his accounting business out of it. We lived there while he built the big one. That's probably where my sister and her husband are sleeping."

"Multiple dwellings, so it's like an official survival compound. I'm feeling scared."

Shane chuckled. "If things ever go south, it will be the people who don't have a place like this that you'll be afraid of."

"Why is that?"

"Because they'll be desperate. And desperate people will do anything to feed their kids or even themselves. Think of it as an in-laws' quarters."

Lilith looked at the freshwater stream flowing into the pond as they drove past. "You're telling me that your dad didn't have a survival compound in mind when he bought this place?"

"I didn't say that. In fact, there's a clearing right above the gate where we came in that could easily fit four to five travel trailers or fifth-wheels. That gate is the only way in or out for a vehicle." Shane cut the engine. "The surrounding ridgelines create a natural fortification all around the property. And that clearing above the gates makes the perfect overwatch position for monitoring approaching visitors."

Lilith opened her door and stepped out. "You're not making me feel any better."

"I don't know why. This is one of the safest places in the world." Shane felt the biting cold of the wind which swirled flurries around his head as he exited the truck.

Shane's father and mother stepped out onto the porch, soon followed by his sister and her husband.

"Lilith, this is my mom and dad, Tonya and Paul." He hugged them, then embraced his little sister. "This is Angela and her husband, Greg."

The warm welcomes and salutations flowed as freely as a mountain stream while Shane and Lilith were ushered inside.

He put his arm around Angela. "When did you get in?"

"Yesterday. It's a good thing, too. The Asheville Airport closed today because of the weather. Looks like you had a little fender bender on the way here. Rough trip?"

Shane looked outside at his truck. "Yeah, but we're here now. All's well that ends well."

Shane's mother retied her apron. "Bring in your things and get settled. Lunch will be ready in about twenty minutes. I made hot browns. Shane, I've set up your old room upstairs for Lilith. You can take the guest room in the basement."

Greg put his hand on Shane's shoulder. "I'll help you bring in your stuff."

"Thanks." Shane zipped up his coat and returned to the blustery winter weather, which continued to get worse.

CHAPTER 2

The U.S. government has a technology, called a printing press or today, its electronic equivalent, that allows it to produce as many U.S. dollars as it wishes at no cost.

Ben Bernanke-Federal Reserve Chairman 2006-2014

Shane relaxed a little after surviving lunch and dinner without a major confrontation between Lilith and his parents.

"Dinner was wonderful, Mrs. Black. Thank you very much." Lilith seemed to be enjoying herself or at least putting on a good show of it.

"My pleasure, Lilith," said Shane's mother. "But please, call me Tonya. Why don't all of you retire to the den? I'll bring some hot cider along in a moment. President Donovan will be issuing his statement to the press about today's market crash at 7:00. I'm sure no one will want to miss it."

Shane offered his hand to Lilith, leading her to the den. They both sat on the large hearth, next to the blazing warm fire.

Angela and Greg took the loveseat while Paul took the couch and waited for his wife to join him.

"How long are you guys staying?" Shane asked Angela.

"Until the 3rd. School isn't back in until the 9th." She put her hand on Greg's leg.

"What grade do you teach?" asked Lilith.

"Kindergarten. I know, it's not rocket science. But I don't think I could handle kids from the higher grades, especially in Las Vegas public schools."

"Don't sell yourself short," laughed Lilith. "Kindergarteners can be brutal."

Shane looked at Greg who had the same monotone expression he always wore. "How are you adjusting to being out of the Air Force?"

"It's going good." His smile was shallow.

Shane attempted to keep the ball in play just a little longer. The surefire way to get a guy talking was to bring up the subject of work. "Angela told me your job is going great. At least it pays well. What exactly does your company do?"

"The company is called Filter. One of my buddies left the Air Force and went to Silicon Valley. He's good with meshing computer processes with human input. He built a couple of his own startups, which never got off the ground, but then one of the big social media giants approached him about starting a company for them to outsource to."

"Big like Facebook?" Shane asked. "Doesn't India usually get most of the outsource work?"

"I can't say who, but you're in the ballpark," Greg answered. "The job is content moderation. It requires a native understanding of the English language and culture. It can't be outsourced to a foreign country. At least not if the company wants accurate moderation.

Basically, our company pulls down posts that our client sees as inappropriate. Cognizant used to have the contract, but the employees started melting down at work."

"Content moderation is stressful?" Shane was confused.

"The employees have strict quotas, and they're essentially watching and taking down ISIS videos, porn, violence, it's pretty hardcore stuff. You'll lose the illusion of living in a polite society after about a week of doing that job. The internet is still largely unpoliced. I'm not claiming that everything we do is right, but we're the ones that keep social media from looking like something off the Dark Web."

"What, exactly, is your role?" Shane asked.

"Glorified babysitter, essentially. As a drone pilot, I had to sit through a lot of compartmentalization training and mandatory counseling after every kill mission. My job is to monitor moderators, pull them away from the screen for a break when they start looking crazy, and try to talk them down with the same psychobabble that the military gave me when I had a hard day at work."

Angela smiled at Shane and Lilith. "Comparatively, kindergarten kids aren't that bad."

Greg's smile seemed a little more genuine. "One thing it has taught me, if society ever breaks down, it will be just like your dad says. Without the thin blue line to hold these monsters back, America will turn into a bad horror movie."

Paul nodded his approval of the statement and turned on the television. "The president should be on in a moment."

Shane took two cups of hot cider from his mother, passing one to Lilith. "Thanks, Mom."

President Tobias Donovan walked to the White House Press Room podium, flanked by a phalanx of top federal officials, including Treasury Secretary Lee Anne Colby, Fed Chairman Jason Walker, FDIC Chair Carter Smith, the Democratic Speaker of the House Warren Ritter, and the Republican Senate Majority leader Melanie Archer. The graveness of the situation was punctuated by this show of force.

Donovan's face lacked his customary smile, as if he regretted what he was about to say. "My fellow citizens, tonight I come to you with a heavy heart. Serious fissures beneath the surface of our financial system have been a concern of mine for decades. Today, we saw a high-magnitude seismic event hit the markets as a result of those cracks deep in the system's crust.

"I won't bore you with a laborious explanation, but in short, historically low-interest rates have forced retirement funds to chase gains in risky assets. When coupled with a monetary supply that has more than doubled in the past decade and a half, equity prices have been pushed to astronomical levels, creating inherent instability in the market.

"Today's losses greatly exacerbated the problem of federal, state, and local pension shortfalls, which currently exceed $14 trillion. I wish that were the only issue we were dealing with. Social Security is also up against the wall. Technically, the program is fully funded for a few more years, but much of those funds have been borrowed against by other programs, and the reality is that the well has gone dry. The Social Security shortfall presently sits at $35 trillion.

"The good folks here at the podium and I have been in meetings with each other and our top advisors since the markets were closed early this afternoon at 1:15 PM."

Donovan looked to his left and right to the Speaker and Senate Majority leader, respectively. "My friends on both sides of the aisle have an ingrained distaste for the word *bailout*, but after today, we all understand that America has to be saved.

"More than a decade ago, the federal government acted swiftly and decisively to bail out the big banks in this country. Insurance agencies and manufacturing companies also received assistance during that period.

"This time, the burden falls squarely on the

shoulders of the American people, through no fault of their own. One of the phrases that came up often in today's meetings was moral hazard. That's a term which describes the risk created by bailing out failed institutions. If you bail out one company because they took on too much risk, you'll have to do the same for others who will take on unnecessary risk simply because they know they'll get a government-funded lifeline if things don't go their way.

"But I argued that the American people don't fit into that model. After we've asked you to prop up banks and financial institutions who've acted recklessly, I believe the true moral hazard is to not help you when you need it most.

"With that said, the size of the relief package necessary to fully backstop every failing program would destabilize the currency. So, we've hashed out a plan that I truly believe is the best we can offer.

"The Fed and Treasury will be working together to issue a combination of loans and quantitative easing programs to prop up our failing state, local, federal, as well as private pension systems at 50 cents on the dollar. If you work for a municipality or private company that is not in trouble, your pension will not be affected.

"We'll be working with those troubled entities to come up with plans which will phase out defined benefit plans and replace them with sustainable 401k-style accounts.

"We'll also backstop Social Security and Medicare at 75 cents on the dollar. We'll begin means testing both programs immediately with a thirty-year phase-out of the programs.

"Our actions are drastic, to be sure. They'll come under tough scrutiny from the pundits. Some will say we've gone too far, and others that we've not gone far enough. But the Emergency Relief Package Act has bipartisan and nearly-unanimous support from both houses of Congress. Believe me when I tell you that it is the best plan we can offer."

Lilith was first to comment. "Fifty cents on the dollar for pensioners and 75 cents on the dollar for Social Security. That's not fair."

Paul held Tonya's hand on the couch. "It wasn't fair to the passengers of the Titanic who paid for an entire voyage but were handed a life jacket halfway across. Yet, the ones who got life vests were the lucky ones in the story."

He turned his attention to his son. "Shane, this is essentially a 40-trillion-dollar infusion of new currency into the system. Markets will probably bounce back heavy on Tuesday. You should try to get out while you can. Get as much cash as possible also."

Lilith interjected, "I'm not sure running around like Chicken Little is the best course of action every time an acorn lands on your head."

Tonya leaned closer to Paul. With her sweet and charming voice, she said, "I'm not sure I'd characterize a 20% drop in the markets and a $40-trillion-dollar bailout as an acorn on the noggin."

Lilith finished her cider and placed the mug on the hearth. "I understand that overreacting is how your family handles perceived threats, but pulling out of stocks all at once might not be the best thing for Shane."

"Excuse me?" Tonya's voice jumped a couple of octaves. "You're a guest in our house and we're Shane's family."

"I might not be family yet, but I'm the official publicist for Backwoods, and I handle Shane's personal affairs. I assure you that I have his best interest at heart. You people won't even go to one of his shows. How do you think that makes him feel?"

Shane gave her hand a squeeze, a subtle cue to back off before it was too late.

However, Paul's eyes showed that the Rubicon had been crossed. "Shane's mother and I don't listen to music that glorifies adultery, drunkenness, nor fornication. He was well aware of our stance long before he moved to Nashville."

"Can you all quit talking about me like I'm not in the room?" Shane stood up. "I'm here for three days. Is it too much to ask that you get along for seventy-two hours?" He offered scolding looks to Lilith and his parents.

Paul's expression showed that he had more to say, but he held his tongue.

"I'm sorry, Shane." Lilith picked up the empty mug to take to the kitchen. "If you'll all excuse me, I think I'll turn in. It's been a long day."

Shane watched her leave the room. "I'm going to bed, too. I'll see you all in the morning."

***

Shane showered and dressed warmly to sleep as the basement was always the coldest room in the cabin. It was still early and he wasn't sleepy, so he scrolled through the headlines about the president's address and the ERPA.

A knock came to the door. "Come in," called Shane.

Paul walked in and took a seat on the foot of the bed. "Are you warm enough down here, Son?"

"Mom's got the covers piled on thick, plus I'm wearing sweatpants and a hoodie."

"We should have tempered our responses to Lilith, but you know how I get when I feel like your mother is being attacked."

"I know. Lilith was out of line. I'll talk to her in the morning."

Paul put his hand on Shane's shoulder. "She mentioned that she wasn't family yet. Are y'all talking about getting married?"

"I've already bought the ring. We're performing in Times Square. I'm going to ask her at the ball drop."

"On national television?"

"Yeah." He smiled at the thought. "She loves that sort of thing."

"What about you? I always thought you liked things more private."

"Yeah, well, I can't exactly escape the limelight at this point."

"You're sure she's the one?"

Shane instantly felt a lump in his throat. He swallowed hard and looked down at his phone.

"She's the one. Lilith is the most beautiful girl I've ever seen. Every time we walk into a room, people stop to look."

"Oh, she's pretty enough. There's no doubt about that." Paul's forehead creased. "However, you'll have to forgive me for my skepticism. That wasn't the most convincing delivery. You hesitated."

Shane took a deep breath, determined not to let emotion overtake him. "You know who *the one* was, Dad."

"Well, Son. You left her behind. What did you expect her to do?"

"I was gone for a month when Julianna married Will. I had no idea! Will was one of my best friends."

"He was friends with Julianna, too. All three of you were on the worship team together." Paul hugged Shane. "But that was seven years ago. It's time you let go."

"That's what I'm trying to do with Lilith."

"Two very different people, Lilith and Julianna. Anyone can tell that just by looking at them."

"I thought you'd be happy that I'm getting married instead of us living together. Besides, I'll never meet anyone else like Julianna."

Paul patted his leg. "Stacking one mistake on top of another isn't going to make anyone happy. And as far as meeting someone like Julianna, you were in church, serving God when you met her. The Bible says to seek first the kingdom of God and His righteousness and all these other things will be added to you.

"You can't expect to run into someone like Julianna in the country music industry. There may have been a time when country music was about family and heritage, but now it's mostly smut, just like everything else the world has to offer.

"If the fame and the fortune aren't doing it for you, you can always turn back to God. I remember the light in your eye when you and Julianna used to play together on Sunday mornings in that high school auditorium."

Shane stared blankly at the back of his phone. "She and Will still lead worship?"

"Yep. Their little boy is getting big, Cole is his name. You'll see them at the Christmas Eve service if they don't cancel it because of the weather.

"Back to what I was saying about the bailout, the M2 money supply is right about $20 trillion. Injecting another $40 trillion triples the available currency. Obviously, its entrance into the economy will be staggered. It will be issued when needed as Social Security and pension payments, but all else being equal, we have to price in a 200 percent increase for inflation. It's hard to say how fast commodity markets will react, but sooner or later, they'll do the math.

"Of course, the wheels have to stay on the bus long enough for that to even matter. Like I said before, we're in uncharted waters when it comes to instability."

"Why would I want to move to cash if inflation is going to skyrocket?"

"Because instability is the bigger monster. Don't stay in all cash. Buy gold, silver, farmland, anything that will survive a complete collapse. I'm talking physical products, not REITs and ETFs."

"Okay, I appreciate the advice."

"Do you carry when you're on the road?"

"No, it's rare that we have a tour that doesn't stop in multiple cities where handguns are banned unless you have a local permit. Those are tough to get. Impossible if you're not a resident. You can possess marijuana in more places than a handgun these days."

"Our forefathers are spinning in their graves." Paul stood up. "I'll let you get some rest. Sleep well, Son."

"Goodnight." Shane watched his father close the door then crawled under the covers and turned off the light.

CHAPTER 3

Fiat currency always eventually returns to its intrinsic value—zero.

Voltaire

Nine days later. Early afternoon, New Year's Eve.

From his hotel room at the Plaza, Shane looked down across the barren trees of Central Park. Remnants of the blizzard, which had swept across the nation, still covered the park in white. The huge pond at the corner of Central Park was frozen, but the wind whipping between the surrounding skyscrapers had pushed the snow back from the ice.

Shane surveyed the streets outlined by pitch-black sludge from the melting snow. His eyes wandered to the Sherman Memorial below. A larger-than-life image of the Union General sat upon a valiant steed, led by a personified likeness of the goddess, Victory. The whole thing glistened in gold like one of the coins designed by the statute's creator, Augustus Saint-Gaudens. Protestors were gathered around the immediate vicinity.

Shane laughed to himself and mumbled aloud, as if addressing the scorched-earth general upon his mount. "I don't know what those people are fussing about, old-timer, but I'm guessing you're safe. Unlike your confederate counterparts. Most of them have been relegated to dark storage dungeons. I suppose it's good to be on the winning side of history."

Shane's father had a modest collection of the $10 Indian Head gold coins as well as the $20 Double Eagle gold coins designed by Saint-Gaudens, so he'd grown up being familiar with the artist's work. His mind darted back to the advice his father had given him before Christmas.

The news played on the television in the background. Shane picked up his phone. He scrolled through his contacts until he came to Butch Werner, his personal financial consultant. Shane dialed the number.

"Shane," Butch answered. "I hope you know that you're the only client I take calls from on Saturdays and New Year's Eve."

Shane laughed. "I hope you know that you're the only financial advisor that I let manage my $3-million-dollar portfolio, despite numerous recommendations from people at the label and friends."

"Touché. What can I do for you, Shane?"

"How much do I have liquid right now? I know we've been letting the payouts from those dividend stocks accrue for a while."

"Give me a second to pull up your account." Butch was silent for a few moments. "Looks like roughly seventy-five thousand. Are you thinking of putting it to work? Now's a good time to buy, S&P, the Dow, everything has bounced back from the Christmas massacre. But I'll tell you who the big winners are from the bailout, it's the REITs that specialize in assisted living facilities. The good ones are up thirty percent from where they were even before the market took a downturn. I've got a line on a couple that are way undervalued."

Shane watched the sun glint off of the statue below. "I appreciate you looking out for me, but I'd like to buy some gold coins."

"Gold is a relic, man. I'd advise against it."

"Must be a lot of cash flowing to relics. It's up $700 from Christmas Eve."

"That's the fear trade. Same thing happened back in the sub-prime crisis. It shot straight toward the sun like Icarus, brushed elbows with $2,000, then plummeted for the next five years. By 2016, it was barely hanging on to $1,000. Once everyone figures out that this bailout money is real, Icarus is going to get his wings burned off for flying too close to the sun again. Gold will crash. I want to save you from that pain."

"What are you talking about? Gold is almost $3,000. Even the people who bought at the top during the previous crisis are sitting pretty."

"Yeah, after a decade of handwringing. You don't want to go through that, trust me."

"I appreciate your advice, but I'm not going to take it. Can you get me some coins?"

"What are you talking about? Coins? I can put you in GLD. Or there's UGL, which is leveraged for 2X returns. If you win, you take twice the profits, but if you lose, you'll get slaughtered. I definitely wouldn't recommend that."

"No, no. I'm not interested in ETFs. I want physical delivery."

"What, like something to carry around in your pocket? Who have you been listening to?"

"Someone who doesn't get paid a percentage of my total portfolio. Can you help me or do I need to start shopping around for a new advisor?"

"Whoa, hang on, Tex. If you want to buy actual coins, you need to go to a dealer. Either a brick-and-mortar shop or one of these online retailers. I can have the cash deposited into your personal checking account on Tuesday, but it probably won't show up until Wednesday or Thursday."

"Wednesday or Thursday? Gold could jump a $1,000 by then."

"You've got cash in the bank, don't you?"

"$50,000 or so, I guess. But I didn't want to use that."

"Then pay with plastic, or better yet, metal. You've got an Amex Black Card. You can buy out Fort Knox. But, if I were you, I'd wait until you get your cash from the dividends. Use it as a cooling off period."

"Thanks, Butch, but I'm sure this is what I want to do. I'd also like to lighten up on everything else. Sell off 20% of my portfolio."

"Twenty percent?" Butch's voice screeched like a cat whose tail had just been caught beneath a rocking chair. "The markets are going gangbusters. This is the wrong time to get out, Shane."

"Once again, I appreciate the advice, but I'll expect the trade confirmations in my email on Tuesday morning. Have a Happy New Year, Butch."

The despair over losing such a large chunk of his commissions reverberated in Butch's voice. "Yeah, Happy New Year, Shane. I'll talk to you next week."

Shane hung up the phone and began looking for online bullion retailers. His search was immediately interrupted by a knock at the door. He checked the peephole and turned the knob. "Hey, how was the trip?"

Derrick and Bridgette Collum came in the room. Like Lilith, Bridgette was in phenomenal shape, well-manicured, dressed in expensive clothes, and had similar flowing blonde hair. Derrick took care of himself, wore shoulder-length brown hair, and generally looked the part of the country music bad boy.

"The flight was fine, the ride from JFK to the hotel was a nightmare!" Bridgette plopped down on the sofa.

"It's New York. It's always a nightmare." Shane sat down at the small gilded writing desk.

"Not like this. Protestors are all over the place,

blocking traffic in some places. The driver had to coordinate with his dispatch center to get us here." Derrick took a seat on the couch next to Bridgette.

"Would have been faster to take the subway," said Shane.

"Yeah, right. And haul all my luggage by myself?" Bridgette rolled her eyes and crossed her legs.

"What were the protestors demonstrating about?" Shane asked.

"Who knows?" Derrick shook his head. "It looks like some reiteration of Occupy Wall Street. Same incoherent messaging. A bunch of signs asking, *Where's my bailout?* People chanting, *This is what the future looks like.* More signs about how old Republicans are sticking young Democrats with the check. And then all kinds of signs that had nothing to do with anything. It's a circus."

"Gas prices have doubled in a week. It was like $7.00 a gallon the last time we stopped to fill up the bus," said Shane.

"I don't think that's worth wasting your New Year's Eve over." Bridgette flipped her hair and crossed her legs in the other direction.

Shane crossed his hands. "When fuel goes up, so will the price of everything else. All the stuff on the shelves gets there by plane, train, or truck, and they all need fuel to move. Working-class people are going to feel this. They are the ones who buy tickets to our shows. If they have to choose between groceries or a ticket to see Backwoods, what do you think is going to get cut from the budget?"

"If it were me, I'd choose you guys." Bridgette

kissed her husband. "But I get what you're saying. Maybe we should all start tightening our belts, just in case." She looked around the room. "Where's Lilith?"

Shane pursed his lips. "Where do you think?"

Bridgette and Derrick looked at each other and said in unison, "The gym."

"Good guess." Shane smiled.

Bridgette clapped her hands. "It's New Year's Eve. Where's the champagne?"

"It's 1:00 in the afternoon on New Year's Eve and we have to perform tonight." Shane eyed her like a three-year-old near a cookie jar.

"Oh, please. A glass of champagne isn't going to kill you. Remember Mariah Carey's show a few years back? You can never butcher New Year's that bad."

"Tonight's the big night. I want the show to go well. Did you find out what slot we're getting?"

"You guys are closing out the old year with *Mud Flaps*, and then *It's a Full Moon Tonight* will be the first song America will hear next year." Bridgette smiled. "And I talked to Ryan. Either he or Jenny will hold the mic for you when you pop the big question."

"Lilith is going to love it!" Shane's face glowed. "Thanks, Bridgette. On second thought, maybe we could have a glass of champagne." Shane picked up the house phone.

"Good afternoon, Mr. Black. How can I help you?"

"I'd like to order two bottles of Cristal. One for now, and I'd like to have a bottle of the rosé waiting in my room after the ball drop."

"Get two bottles for now!" Bridgette added.

"Make that two for now and one for later."

"I'd be happy to, Mr. Black, but I should inform you, all of our imports have gone up."

"Gone up? By how much?"

"Regretfully, double, sir. The dollar has taken a big hit against foreign currencies. I'm afraid it's beyond our control."

Shane quickly realized it wasn't only the working class who'd be taking a hit. "So $2,400 for a bottle of Cristal Rosé and $1,200 for the regular Cristal?"

"Yes, sir."

Shane looked at Bridgette. "Is Veuve okay for you?"

"Sure, but you better keep that bottle of rosé for Lilith tonight."

Shane modified his selections. "Alright, we'll take two bottles of Veuve for now, and the Cristal Rosé for tonight."

"Very well, sir. I'll send it right up."

The door lock clicked, then Lilith walked in wearing her yoga pants and workout top. "Hey, girlfriend!"

Bridgette got up from the couch and approached her for a hug. "Hey, sweetie!"

Lilith held up one finger. "Better hold that thought until I get a shower. I'm a sweaty mess."

"Sure," Bridgette said.

"How was Christmas?" Derrick asked.

Lilith looked at him as if he were joking. "Seriously? Shane didn't tell you?"

"No, what happened?" Bridgette drew her brows together.

Lilith went into the bathroom and ran the shower so it could heat up. "His folks didn't like me. We had to leave a day early."

"What?" asked Bridgette.

"We left Christmas Day, right after breakfast. I'll be out in a few minutes." Lilith closed the door.

"Ouch." Derrick set his teeth together and looked at Shane.

"It wasn't that bad. We were going to leave the day after Christmas anyway." Shane lifted his shoulders and returned his task of looking for gold coin dealers online.

"You couldn't survive the full three days and had to pull out early." Bridgette stared at him. "You don't think that's bad?"

"It could have been worse." He sighed and stood up from the small writing desk. "The champagne will be up in a minute. I've got to run down to the lobby for a second. Lilith will probably want to go eat when she gets out. You guys are welcome to come with us."

"Sure, we'll come," said Derrick.

"Better hurry." Bridgette gave a sneaky smile and raised her eyebrows. "That champagne might not last long."

Shane walked out of the room and continued looking at his phone while he made his way to the elevator. "Wow! These coins are selling for a lot more than the gold price." He compared prices with several other online dealers on his way down to the lobby. Once there, Shane took a seat to add several coins to his cart only to find that they were out of stock. He quickly navigated back to the second-best-priced dealer which had many more listings but soon realized very few of the offerings were still available.

Shane put in a call to his father.

"Hello."

"Dad, hey, I'm looking for some gold coins online, but it seems most everything is sold out. What's available is almost 50 percent higher than the stated gold price. Why is that?"

"It's a run on gold. Premiums have shot up since the bailout announcement."

"Do you think they'll go back down?"

"No, Son. I think they'll keep rising until no bullion is available at all. We could see 100 percent premiums where gold is at $4000 and a one-ounce coin is going for $8000. When the central banks began suppressing the gold price after the last run-up, gold got so cheap that many of the miners went out of business. But I think the price will eventually catch up with the premiums. You should take anything that's still available at this point. Some of the big dealers offer faster shipping for an added charge or on certain products. Spend the extra money to get your order as soon as possible. This house of cards is about to come tumbling down.

"Come on home as soon as you realize you need to. Don't hesitate."

"What do you mean as soon as I realize I need to?" Shane thought the comment odd, even for his overly-cautious father.

"The economy is in a classic melt up, just like

the Weimar Republic. America is going to get more and more dangerous from here. The best time to come home would be right now. The second best time would be when you come to terms with reality and realize it's your only choice. Bring Lilith with you. We'll learn to get along—in time. She can live in the little house until you get married. Then, the two of you can live there. Angela and Greg can move into the main cabin with us."

"Angela and Greg aren't going back to Vegas?"

"They haven't made up their minds yet. They still have a couple more days before their flight but Mom and I are all but begging them to stay."

"Okay, thanks."

"I love you, Son. You'll always be welcome here as long as you respect our rules. You always have, so I'd expect nothing different."

"I appreciate that, Dad. I love you, too. Happy New Year."

"I'm doubtful of that. I think this will be the worst year this nation has ever seen. You take care of yourself."

"I will. Bye." Shane felt very unsettled about the urgency in his father's voice. Shane finally found a handful of European coins minted prior to 1933. He loaded up his cart and quickly entered his credit card information. Once he'd received confirmation of the order, he scrolled through the site looking for more available coins. Shane added two over-priced gift sets from Cameroon and a few coins with unsightly animals such as rats and monkeys from Singapore. All of the coins like those of his father's, which he'd grown up looking at, were sold out. No eagles, buffalos, maple leaves, or any of the beautiful coins designed by Saint-Gaudens were available. Shane completed his purchase and walked to the lobby entrance. He looked toward the Sherman Memorial to see the small gaggle of protestors was growing.

He turned around to locate the hotel's ATM. "I should have gone by the bank before we left Nashville." Shane pulled out his debit card and hurried to the machine. "I should have done a lot of things." He slid his card into the reader and entered his PIN. He frowned to see that $500 was the limit for a daily withdraw. The corners of his mouth fell even further when the machine dispensed his cash in all twenty-dollar-bills.

Disappointed that he'd not fared better in his quest, Shane returned to the elevator and went back to his room.

When he opened the door, the sound of laughter, merriment, and mirth met him. Derrick, Bridgette, and Lilith all had a sparkling glass of holiday cheer.

"Shane's dad is a hoot." Lilith slugged back the last of her glass and began pouring herself another. "What did he call it, honey? Something like the vibrating cup of water in Jurassic Park; you know, the scene right before the tyrannosaurus attacks? This guy is a master of hyperbole. I don't know how Shane got out in as good of a condition as he did. His dad thinks the Christmas massacre was just a precursor to the big one."

Shane decided he wouldn't discuss the purchase he'd just made with his soon-to-be fiancé. "Are we going to eat?"

"Sure. Let's polish off this bottle and go." Lilith poured the last glass of champagne for Shane.

CHAPTER 4

The problem with socialism is that eventually, you run out of other people's money.

Margaret Thatcher

Shane stood near his hotel room window, dressed and ready for the Times Square New Year's Eve show. He looked down from the eighth floor of the Plaza Hotel at the gathering of protestors. Their numbers had tripled since lunch. He glanced at his watch. "It's past eight o' clock. We should get going soon." Shane snuck a peek at the three-carat diamond ring in his front jeans pocket.

Lilith, called from the bedroom, "Five more minutes."

Shane took out his phone and called Bobby, his

head of security, who was staying several blocks down at the Knickerbocker Hotel. Stan, the other security coordinator, Casey, Backwoods' drummer, and Miguel who played bass guitar were also staying right in Times Square.

"Hey, boss. What's up?" answered Bobby.

"Is everything set up down there?" Shane ran his hand through his thick, jet-black hair, checking himself in the mirror once more.

"Yeah, we dropped off the equipment. Their people said they'd handle the setup. It ain't like one of our shows where it's just you guys and an opening act. Lots of different performers coming and going throughout the night. But they seem like they know what they're doing."

Shane smiled. "Like they've done this before?"

Bobby laughed, "Yeah, something like that."

"If you and Stan aren't busy, do you think you could come up to the hotel and walk us to the studios? We've got a revolution brewing up here."

"They're all over the city. I'm staying plugged into the situation. NYPD is keeping an eye on the demonstrations, but evidently, the mayor wants the police to stand down unless they start hurting people. I'll be in your lobby in about fifteen minutes. Are you planning on walking?"

"It's less than a mile. I can't imagine there'd be a faster way to traverse New York City on New Year's Eve."

"The N train would take you straight to the studios, but it wouldn't be any faster. It might save a few steps if the ladies are wearing heels. The biggest problem is that we'd be in a confined space if something popped off with these protestors while we're underground."

"Bridgette and Lilith are both accustomed to wearing heels. I'm sure they'll be fine walking. See you downstairs."

A knock came to the door. Shane opened it for Derrick and Bridgette. "Bobby and Stan are going to escort us to the green room." Shane let them in and closed the door behind them.

"Why, are the protestors getting violent?" Derrick asked.

Lilith called from the bedroom, "I told you, Shane's father has him convinced that the end is nigh."

Shane held back the curtains for Bridgette and Derrick to look down at the street. "That group right there is in all black; run-of-the-mill rabble-rousers, I suppose. Over by the big gold statue is about twenty people with Antifa markings, sickle-and-hammer bandanas, red and black flags, red stars, red armbands. I saw a few Guy Fawkes masks. It's a general hodge-podge of ne'er-do-wells."

Bridgette held tightly to Derrick's arm. "I think I'll feel safer if Bobby and Stan are with us."

"Don't let him poison you with that stuff, Bridgette. It's contagious." Lilith came into the room wearing black skin-tight jeans, a gold-sequined long-sleeve top, which bared her toned shoulders and hung low in the back. Her golden blonde hair was blown out with gentle waves, and she held a black leather jacket over her arm.

Shane gazed upon her sculpted figure, full lips, and mesmerizing eyes. Even after all this time, she still took his breath away. He felt sure he'd never seen a woman more beautiful. All her teasing about his paranoia melted into the background. "Ready?"

"Let's go!" She took his arm and the group made their way to the elevator.

Once in the lobby, they met up with the security team. Stan was muscular with dark, crew cut hair. Bobby was a towering wall of a man, 6'8" and close to three hundred pounds.

"Any news?" Shane asked.

Bobby shook his head. "I overheard some officers talking about it. They're calling the movement Occupy the Future."

"What the heck is that supposed to mean?" Lilith inquired.

Bobby shrugged. "I don't know. Something about the children being our future I guess. It's mostly young people. I suppose they feel like they're getting stuck with the bill for the Social Security and pension bailout. It's mostly for retired or soon-to-be retired folks."

"With seven-dollar gas, the future does look pretty bleak to someone barely getting by." Shane put his arm around Lilith as they walked down the stairs of the hotel into the street.

The chants coming from the protestors were loud but un-unified. Bobby kept himself between the demonstrators and the rest of the group.

Bridgette shouted out, "Yeah, seven-dollar gas and twenty-four hundred for a bottle of Cristal. Maybe we should be over there with them."

Shane knew she'd meant it as a light-hearted joke, but he figured even the super-rich would soon be feeling the economic pinch. The group walked briskly through the cavernous streets of New York City to the ABC studios where the GMA green room had been transformed to host the performers for the New Year's Eve show. Once inside, Lilith and Bridgette quickly split off to rub elbows with the other celebrities. Shane and Derrick rendezvoused with Casey and Miguel.

"Anything good to eat?" Shane asked the drummer.

Casey replied, "Those little steak thingys on a stick are pretty good. The sushi might have been great at three o'clock, but it's a little warm."

Shane wrinkled his nose. "Thanks for the warning." He made his rounds saying hello to the other people in the music industry that he recognized but keeping to himself as much as possible.

The show's host came up to Shane. "Shane Black, love your music. Your manager, Bridgette, told me you're going to pop the big question tonight."

"Good to meet you, Ryan." Shane shook his hand. "Yeah, she said you could help me out with that."

"Absolutely. I'm going to send Jenny over to discuss the details with you. She'll be upset if I don't cut her in on that. She loves doing the engagements. Let me or Jenny know if you need anything."

Shane waved. "I appreciate it."

The night moved on smoothly, but Shane only had one thing on his mind. He wanted the proposal to be perfect.

Finally, at 11:45, Backwoods got their cue to go to the stage. Shane picked up his guitar as he had so many times before. Casey set the beat by clicking his drumsticks then the band jammed through their award-winning song, *Mud Flaps*. When they finished the song, the hosts, Jenny and Ryan, joined them on the stage.

Ryan stood by Shane. "Backwoods, what a great song! I know there are a couple of ladies who travel with the band, your manager Bridgette Collum and PR Coordinator Lilith Taylor. Why don't you call them on up here to count down the ball drop with us?"

Shane waved for the girls to come up on the stage.

Ryan handed the mic to Jenny.

Jenny fixed her thick black scarf to shield her neck from a chilling breeze. "With Derrick being married, the title of band heartthrob has been handed to you, Shane. I hear you're getting ready to break a lot of single girls' hearts right now." She held the mic for Shane.

Lilith looked bewildered by the statement. Shane's heart beat in his chest. He never felt nervous on stage, but his mouth suddenly went dry and his hand shook so bad he feared he might drop the ring. Nevertheless, he pulled the large gemstone from his pocket. "Lilith, you're the love of my life. Will you marry me?"

Her eyes widened as she looked at the magnificent diamond sparkling in the bright stage lights. She covered her mouth and nodded emphatically. Shane pulled her glove off and slipped the ring on her finger.

Jenny held the mic to Lilith. "Was that a yes?"

"Yes!" she said, looking at Shane. She turned to the mic and the camera. "Yes!"

The crowd had already started the countdown. "Ten, nine, eight…"

All around the crowd, the protestors had gathered in the streets. Their chants grew louder, drowning out the revelers' countdown to midnight. "Where's my bailout? Where's my future? Where's my bailout? Where's my future?"

Shane watched the ball go down and the seconds count off on the giant screen, but the cheers of Happy New Year were overwhelmed by the chants of the protestors.

The chants grew louder while the DJ played the required Auld Lang Syne. "Where's my bailout? Where's my future?"

Even so, the show must go on. The customary ringing in of the New Year via the familiar classic finished. Casey clicked his drum sticks together once more and Backwoods performed their latest Grammy winner, *It's a Full Moon Tonight*. Shane tried to concentrate, but could still hear the chants over the blaring speakers all around him.

The merry-making crowd, which had been so enthralled by the band's last song, became more distracted by the protestors. Backwoods finished the song and Bobby came to the stage. He pulled Derrick and Shane close. "I recommend skipping the Hard Rock after party tonight. The protestors are breaking bottles and setting cars on fire."

"What do you think?" Derrick asked.

Shane nodded. "Let's get out of here." He waved for Lilith to come over to him. "We're going to head back to the hotel."

"The hotel?" Lilith protested. "We just got engaged! Don't you want to celebrate?"

"We can have a toast at the hotel bar." Shane took her hand and followed Bobby down the stairs.

"You want to party with a bunch of stiffs at the Rose Club? I promise it will be nothing like the soiree at the Hard Rock." Lilith followed defiantly like a child not ready to leave the zoo.

"We need to get off the streets. Backwoods pays Bobby to keep us safe. We can't expect him to do his job if we don't take his advice." Shane looked at the drummer and bass player. "You guys are welcome to come with us."

Miguel shook his head. "Our hotel is right around the corner. If things get dicey we can be there in five minutes."

"Do you want Stan to stay with you?" Derrick asked.

"We'll be fine." Casey waved his hand dismissively.

"Let's keep moving." Bobby ushered Shane's group forward. "We'll cut through the studio and come out on West 44th. I want to take 6th Ave. back to the hotel. Hopefully, it will have fewer protestors than Broadway or 7th Ave."

"Won't that mean less police presence?" Bridgette asked.

"Yeah, but they've been told to stand down unless people are being hurt. By the time the cops are authorized to do anything, it might be too late." Bobby held the door open to the ABC studios.

Shane watched the people still lingering about in the green room as they walked past. They seemed oblivious to the fact that the protests were on the verge of becoming full blown riots.

CHAPTER 5

A number of the things we were forced to do during the crisis made the problem worse.

Hank Paulson-US Treasury Secretary 2006-2009

Shortly after they passed 53rd Street, a young man brushed up against Shane. "Hey bro! They just broke into the currency exchange store! Come on, we might get some foreign currency that will actually buy something!"

Shane held up a hand and kept walking. "Thanks, but I'm good."

With his free hand, the young man pulled down his bandana to reveal his expression of mock surprise. "You're good? What? You don't need any more money? Hey guys, I think we just found some one-percenters." His other hand held a length of metal pipe.

Several of the thugs who were obviously in his crew stopped what they were doing and began to circle around Shane's group. All held various items which could be used as weapons.

"Look we don't want any problems." Bobby stepped closer to the man who was doing all the talking. Stan stood next to Bobby at an angle.

The young punk instinctively stepped back. "Oh, the big man don't want no problems. What? They got you workin' for 'em? You need to get back on the right team." From what the goon probably considered a safe distance, he pointed the pipe at Bobby.

Bobby lunged forward and snatched the pipe.

Without thinking, Shane grabbed hold of the tire iron in the hand of the ruffian nearest him. Shane wrestled the vandal to the ground, twisting and pulling at the make-shift weapon. From the corner of his eye, he could see that Stan and Derrick had also joined in the melee. Shane rolled with the man in the street, claiming the top. He sprawled his leg outward to brace himself and maintain his position. He jerked at the tire tool, then released one hand to send his elbow into the thug's mouth. Shane hammered at the man's face with one elbow while his opposite hand struggled to control the tire iron. Finally, the man let go of the instrument to shield his face from further injury.

Shane felt the toes of two more assailants against his ribs. He swung the tire iron, catching one of his attackers by the ankle and pulling him to the ground. He rolled away from the other goon and scrambled to his feet. He held the tire iron up to block a blow from the hood's baseball bat. He successfully avoided taking a direct hit to the face, but the force of the impact knocked the tire tool from his hands. The metal instrument clanged against the pavement. Shane looked up to see the menacing smile of the thug who held the bat high in the air for another strike. Left with nothing else to protect his face from the blow, Shane crossed his arms above his head.

WHACK! Blood shot sideways from the back of the hooligan's skull. His body trailed laterally behind the spray of dark red fluid.

Shane looked up to see Bobby holding the metal pipe in his hand. Bobby pointed north with the pipe. "Shane, Derrick, get the girls and go!"

Shane looked around to see six of the assailants lying on the ground. Derrick and Stan appeared uninjured. Lilith and Bridgette embraced each other in the center of the area which had become the site of a quick skirmish. Unfortunately, a larger troop of attackers was closing in all around them.

Shane hated to abandon Bobby and Stan, but his first responsibility was to get Lilith to safety. Derrick pulled Bridgette by the arm and began running, keeping her on the opposite side of the conflict. Shane grabbed Lilith's hand and tugged. "Come on!"

He rapidly caught up to Derrick. "Let's cut over to 5th. It can't be any worse than this."

"Lead the way," Derrick agreed.

Shane looked back to see how Bobby and Stan were holding up against the gang of ten or so additional roughnecks. Bobby was swinging the pipe and had already taken down two of them. Stan had another one of them in a choke hold.

"I think they'll be okay. Let's move."

Shortly after turning onto West 54th, the group came upon a fight between private security guards and a criminal group trying to gain access to the Museum of Modern Art. Eight police officers on horseback quickly came to assist the security guards, but three protestors grabbed one of the mounted police and pulled him from his horse. They quickly wrestled his gun away from him and a firefight ensued between the protestors and the remaining seven officers. Another of the cops was dragged from his mount, then another was shot in the head and fell.

Shane saw no less than eight protestors lying on the ground. "We have to get out of here! Run! As fast as you can!"

A brigade of NYPD officers in full riot gear charged on foot in their direction, evidently to respond to the downed officers.

"Get close to the buildings, and keep running. We've got four blocks to go before we get back to the hotel."

Two blocks later, they reached Trump Tower where another skirmish between protestors, police and private security was taking place. The skyscraper had become an epicentric symbol of the clash between capitalism and far-left socialism.

"Don't take time to look. Just keep moving!" Shane led Lilith by the arm. She appeared stunned, as if in shock.

When they reached 58th, Shane yelled, "This way. We'll go in the back. We need to stay away from the protestors in Grand Army Plaza!"

Shane rushed Lilith up the red-carpeted stairs to a locked door. The doorman from inside shook his head. "Sorry, folks. The hotel is closed."

Shane quickly retrieved his room card and held it to the glass. "We're guests! You have to let us in!"

The doorman nodded with a grave expression and quickly unlocked the door. "Pardon me, sir, but I'm sure you understand."

"No problem." Once his group was safely inside, Shane watched the man relock the door. "Come on, let's get upstairs to the room."

Once there, Shane opened the door and let the others in first. He looked at the gold bucket with a white cloth napkin tied around the top of the gold-foiled top of the bottle. It reminded him of the celebration which had been canceled by the rioting. In the back of his mind, he hoped it wasn't an omen of how his life with Lilith would shake out over the years. He wondered if she were considering the same thing.

At present, she seemed to be thinking about nothing but the champagne. She quickly removed the cloth napkin, the gold foil, and pulled the cork. The quintessential pop didn't herald the joyous occasion for which it had been intended. Instead, it served as a $2400 sedative to ease the pain of the traumatic journey from Times Square to the Plaza Hotel. Lilith tried drinking from the bottle but foam spewed from the top causing her to unleash a stream of expletives. She quickly remedied the situation by pouring herself a glass into one of the provided water glasses which held more than the narrow champagne flute. She passed the bottle to her sister-in-arms, plopped down on the couch and began to cry.

Shane took a seat next to her and put his arm around her. He tried to comfort her while simultaneously calling Bobby's phone. No one answered. Next, he tried Stan's, but it also went straight to voicemail. "Call me when you get this. Let me know that you guys are okay."

"No answer?" asked Derrick.

Shane shook his head. He turned to Lilith and used the sleeve of his shirt to wipe the streams of mascara running down her face. "Do you mind if I turn on the news? Will it upset you?"

"No, I can handle watching it, I just can't deal with seeing people getting killed right in front of me." She stood up. "I'm going to go wash my face anyway. I'm sure I look atrocious." Lilith refilled her water glass with champagne and went to the bathroom.

Shane turned on the television and refused the bottle when Bridgette offered it to him. "No thanks. I need to stay clear headed."

"What are you thinking about?" Derrick watched Shane click through the channels.

"We should get out of here first thing in the morning. All this will probably die down at first light, but people are off work for the next two days, so the city could have more rioting tomorrow evening."

"Our tickets are for the second," said Derrick,

"But y'all get on out of here if you can."

"You should forget about your plane tickets. Ride on the tour bus with the rest of us."

"It'll be cramped," Derrick replied.

"We'll make do." Shane paused from surfing when he reached a station covering the riots.

A reporter who'd been covering the festivities in Times Square had quickly shifted gears. "Downtown Manhattan is in utter chaos right now. Police are telling us that massive protests have the entire city under siege, and they are being told to stand down except in situations where human life is at stake.

"Small pockets of demonstrators upset about rising food and fuel prices have been cropping up since the bailout announcement last week, but no one could have guessed such a wave of violence and destruction could ignite so quickly. Authorities are reporting multiple attacks against police and the public. Gangs of criminals are using the protests as cover to commit greater crimes such as breaking into high-end shops, stealing cash registers, and looting businesses. With the mayor's stand-down order, they can act with virtual impunity except in cases where private security contractors are involved."

"That's what we witnessed at the Met." Bridgette chugged a glass of bubbles from an actual champagne flute. "Can you imagine if they get inside? Most of those paintings are worth over a million."

Shane's knuckles were white from the angst. To him, Bobby and Stan were worth more than every piece of art in that museum. Stan had been with the band for three years, and Bobby had worked with them since their first headline show, over five years ago. Shane tried calling Bobby's phone once more, but still, no answer came.

Next, he called Casey.

"Shane, what's up? Did you guys get to the hotel okay?"

"We did, but Stan and Bobby had to handle some business. Have either of you guys talked to them since we left?"

"No, what happened?"

Shane explained the incident on 6th Ave. "We're going to try to leave a day early. You and Miguel should get back to the hotel soon. Get some rest and be ready to roll out by 7:00 AM."

"What if Stan and Bobby still aren't back by then?"

"They'll be back. They know how to take care of themselves." Shane wished he could convince himself of what he was trying to sell to Casey.

Shane spent the next hour calling hospitals, the jail, as well as Stan's and Bobby's phones, but to no avail.

"You should call Barry and let him handle this," said Derrick.

"Barry is a Nashville attorney. What good can he do in New York?" asked Shane.

"He's got people all over the country. Just call him."

Shane looked at his phone. "Think he'll be up?"

"It's an hour earlier back home. They just finished ringing in the New Year. Barry is up."

Reluctantly, Shane dialed the number.

"Shane! Happy New Year." Barry spoke loudly over the music in the background. "I saw your show. You boys did great. Sorry about the folks up there coming unhinged. Oh, and congratulations on the engagement. You won't find a prettier girl than Lilith. I'm at a party down the street from your house in Belle Meade. Trey and some other folks from the label are here.

"You all okay? Looks like people are getting restless up there."

"That's why I'm calling. We had some trouble on the way home. I can't get in touch with Bobby and Stan." Shane explained what had happened.

"Say no more. Should I wait until morning to call if it's late when I hear something?"

"No," said Shane. "Wake me up. I don't care what time it is. I probably won't sleep anyway."

Once the champagne was gone, Derrick and Bridgette left. Shane took a shower then lay in the bed next to Lilith watching coverage of the riots. The alcohol worked its magic on Lilith and she went to sleep. Shane also eventually drifted off.

CHAPTER 6

And moreover I saw under the sun the place of judgment, that wickedness was there; and the place of righteousness, that iniquity was there. I said in mine heart, God shall judge the righteous and the wicked: for there is a time there for every purpose and for every work.

Ecclesiastes 3:16-17

Shane's phone rang at 5:30 AM. "Hello?" He got out of bed and went into the living area of the junior suite, hoping to not wake Lilith.

"Shane, I'm afraid I've got some bad news." Barry Rothstein's voice sounded more sober and less energetic than it had a few hours earlier.

Shane sat on the sofa. "Go ahead."

"Bobby is being charged with multiple counts of

manslaughter. I guess he took out several of those guys on the street."

"Took out as in killed?"

"Five so far. Two more are in critical condition. If they die, he'll get two additional counts added. They took him to Mount Sinai to treat his injuries. Seems like he didn't get out unscathed. The hospital is understaffed and overworked, so it could be a while before they even get to him. From there, he'll be taken to Central Booking, then to Riker's. I've got the bondsman lined up, but they can't do anything until he's processed in. Even then, he won't be allowed to leave the city until he's cleared. My guy in New York will file a motion to dismiss based on the grounds that it was self-defense."

"What are the odds of that?"

"Pretty good, seeing that it's the truth and that he's got the best criminal defense attorney in New York. But it all depends on the judge."

"Did you hear anything about Stan yet?"

"Yeah." Barry paused. "He's dead."

Shane's stomach sank.

"I'm taking care of everything. Once the coroner does what he needs to do, I'll have the body flown back to Nashville."

"Thanks, Barry."

"The wheels are in motion for Bobby. We can't do anything more for him now. I'll call you when I hear something. I'm going to get some sleep. I've been up all night working on this."

"Sure thing. Thanks, Barry." Shane hung up and sighed, feeling the grief and guilt knowing that Stan had lost his life so they could get away.

He stood up and looked out the window. To his surprise, protestors were still gathered around the Sherman Memorial. None held signs, and no one chanted, but they were there. In typical Occupy fashion, they'd set up tents. One had a camping stove and appeared to be making coffee. Unlike scenes Shane remembered from the previous Occupy demonstrations, the people he could see below looked less fringe. While most still displayed telltale signs of being from the left, they appeared more mainstream than participants from the first iteration of the movement.

Shane's phone vibrated. He looked to see he had a text from the bass guitar player, Miguel. *Don't think we'll be able to leave at 7:00. Any news on Bobby and Stan?*

The answer was far too involved for a text reply. Shane called him back. "Hey, man. Bad news about Bobby and Stan." He relayed everything he knew so far.

Shane waited while Miguel informed Casey, then asked, "What makes you think we can't get out of here at seven?"

Miguel replied, "Turn on the local news. The protestors are blocking off the bridges and tunnels. The news is calling it a siege."

With the situation in a death spiral, Shane wished he'd never come to New York. "Okay, I'll call you back in a while."

Lilith came and stood by him. "I heard you talking about Stan and Bobby. I'm sorry."

He continued to stare out the window. "Yeah, I feel so guilty, but I don't know what else I could have done. Derrick and I had to get you and Bridgette out of there."

"Don't beat yourself up. Stan and Bobby knew what they were signing up for when they took the job. Unfortunately, these things happen. You did the right thing.

"What did Miguel have to say?"

"He told me to turn on the news." Shane scanned the room for the remote. "He thinks it might be hard to get the tour bus out of the city today." He turned on the television and sat down.

A local reporter was at the entrance of the Holland Tunnel where an encampment similar to the one outside his window had popped up. The male reporter had found a pretty young protestor to interview. "Good morning, do you want to tell us who you are and why you're here?"

"Sure." The girl smiled at the camera. "My name is Teresa, and I'm at the Holland Tunnel in case it rains or snows. If the weather gets bad we can just go inside. The people occupying the bridges have the tougher job."

The reporter held back a laugh, as though he'd mistaken her for someone more intellectual. Nevertheless, he gave her one more shot at the interview. "That's smart, but I meant why did you choose to come protest?"

"Oh, like more existentially." The pretty young blonde put her hand over her mouth. "I'm so embarrassed. Um, yes. I'm here because my whole life I've been fed a line of garbage about the American dream. I moved here from Pennsylvania.

I grew up in a working-class family that taught me no one owes me anything, but if I worked hard I could be anything I wanted to be. So, I wanted to be an actress and start my career on Broadway. I slave all week as a waitress so I can run around on my off day and do auditions. My schedule is brutal, but I make it happen.

"Then, last week, Merry Christmas, all the prices at the grocery started going up. Milk is up two dollars! In a week! I live in the city so I can't afford a car, but I'm sure those fuel prices are going to hit the train fares sooner or later. I'm no economist, and I don't really understand exactly how everything is happening, but I know it's because the people who are retiring got bailed out and now my generation is going to foot the bill.

"Folks, I've got news for you, my generation was barely getting by as it was. Now? We're just plain finished. And I'm not going to kill myself to have absolutely nothing to show for it. I can sit here in my tent and do that. And this is way easier."

"I can't argue with that." The reporter seemed relieved that the interviewee had redeemed herself with an intelligible response. "This is Mack Stevens with Channel 6 live in SoHo. Back to you, Michelle."

"So I guess we're not going anywhere today." Lilith walked toward the bedroom.

"If this is going on all over the city, I guess not." Shane slumped forward holding the remote with both hands.

"I'm going to get a shower. Can you call room

service and order some breakfast?"

"Sure." Shane turned down the volume and picked up the in-room phone. "Hi, room service please."

The woman on the other end had a thick Spanish accent. "I'm sorry, room service is busy right now. Nobody coming to work today. Everybody here stay from yesterday."

"You mean the next shift didn't come in?" Shane asked for clarification.

"Yes, everybody living in New Jersey or Brooklyn, maybe Queens. Can't come. Bridges is closed. The people working over here can't live in Manhattan."

"I understand. What about Palm Court? Is the restaurant open?"

"Yes. Is open, pero maybe don't have too many foods. No muffin, no bagel, no croissant, no breads. The bakery can't come."

"Don't they have any bread from yesterday?"

"No. Throw it out. Every day is fresh."

"Every day except today."

"Yes, sir."

"Okay, thanks. I'll come down and see what they have."

"Okay, and maybe check it out the food hall downstairs. Could be somebody is opening."

"Thank you." Shane hung up. He dug a pair of jeans out of his suitcase and shook the wrinkles out of a clean plaid shirt. He knocked on the door of the bathroom. "I've got to go downstairs for breakfast. None of the workers came in today."

"Of course not. They're camping on the

bridges," Lilith yelled over the sound of the shower.

Shane called Derrick on the way to the elevator and filled him in on the latest.

Once downstairs, he wrapped up the conversation and walked to the hostess stand of the opulent restaurant. It was unattended. Shane saw several people sitting at the bar beneath an exquisite stained-glass ceiling. He walked up and took a seat.

Shane smiled at the woman next to him. "Is anyone working the bar?"

"Yeah, there's a couple of people on, but I think they're overwhelmed."

A girl sprinted from the back carrying two plates. She sat them down in front of the people next to Shane. "Hi, can I help you?"

"Um, yes, please. What's easy? And what's available?"

She smiled at Shane and smelled of alcohol. "I appreciate that. I'm the bartender from the Rose Club. I work night shift and had no idea I'd be working this morning. The chef . . ." She rolled her eyes up. "Well, the guy cooking this morning made up a big batch of breakfast potatoes. Scrambled eggs seem to be his specialty. Granola, cereal, we have some fruit but nothing that has to be cut up. Sorry, no bread. Unless you want pancakes."

"Pancakes sound great. I'll take some eggs, potatoes, fruit, and some granola. And throw in whatever breakfast meat is available, sausage, bacon, ham, whatever. Could you possibly box that up for me?"

The hungover attendant wrote everything down. "Even better."

"Great, make it enough for four people. And put a bloody mary on my tab for yourself. You look like you could use it."

The girl giggled. "Yes, sir."

Shane got up from the bar stool. "I'll be back in a few minutes. I'm going to run downstairs and see if they have anything."

"I'll be here." The girl scurried off.

Shane's first stop was the ATM. He grunted at the thought of having another five-hundred-dollars' worth of twenty-dollar bills. He slid his card and entered his PIN. "You're kidding me!" The machine was empty.

Shane felt even more agitated as he descended to the lower level where the Plaza Food Hall was located.

***

Nearly an hour had passed when Shane got back to the room. He placed an assortment of bags on the small coffee table.

"Where were you? I was worried." Lilith was dressed and had her makeup on. "Why did you get so much food?"

"Derrick and Bridgette are coming. Plus, I wanted to make sure we had something to eat over the next day or so, in case we're stuck here for a while."

"What did you get?" Lilith rummaged through the bags.

"I got breakfast from the Palm Court, which had hardly anyone working the kitchen or the front of the house. While I was waiting for that, I went to the food hall downstairs. Only a couple of the little kiosks were open. One was a French bakery. The guy, François, and his helper were pumping out fresh bread so I got a few loaves of that. I have a feeling the sub shop will be short on bread when and if they open up for lunch, but maybe I can buy some cold cuts. We can use that to make our own sandwiches on the baguettes."

"Whoa! Take it easy, Tex. Most people have resolutions to lose weight for the New Year. If we eat all of this, we'll be as big as Bobby."

Shane winced at being reminded of Bobby's terrible predicament. "If deliveries quit coming into the city, this might be all we have to choose from."

Shane heard Derrick's familiar rap against the door. He opened it.

"Hey, the mayor is giving a press conference in five minutes." Derrick walked in and assumed control of the remote.

"You guys got breakfast?" Bridgette asked.

"Yeah." Shane apprised them of the selections. "I bought plenty for everybody. Help yourself."

"Do you think the mayor will act to clear the bridges and tunnels so we can get out of here?" asked Lilith.

"We'll soon find out." Derrick took one of the Styrofoam boxes from Bridgette and began eating.

Shane broke into another of the boxes and turned up the volume.

Mayor Greenwell stood with the police commissioner at his side. "I want to thank the press for coming out today, and I want to thank the NYPD for their difficult task of working all night and on through the morning. We've got some officers who have been on shift for more than eighteen hours at this point.

"I was elected by the people of New York because of my staunch commitment to progressive politics. The thing about values is that you can't only adhere to them when it's convenient.

"I was at Sproul Hall at Berkeley in 1964 when Mario Savio gave his famous speech. That day, I became convinced that indeed sometimes the operation of the machine does become so odious that it makes us sick. Sometimes we have no other choice but to put our bodies upon the gears and upon the wheels, upon the levers, upon all the apparatus, and we have to make it stop! And we have to indicate to the people who run it, that unless we're included in the decision-making process, unless we're given a modicum of respect, allowed to even exist on what's left over after capitalism has robbed us blind, the machine will be prevented from working at all."

Bridgette's brow creased and she pointed at the screen. "This guy does realize that this whole crisis is because we bailed out Social Security, doesn't he? I mean, wasn't that part of FDR's Socialist utopia?"

"Let's listen." Derrick put his finger to his mouth.

Mayor Greenwell continued, "The Occupy the

Future demonstrators have a justifiable grievance and I will not move against them. I will not violate their solemn right, no, their imperative duty to make their voices known. I've instructed the Police Commissioner to maintain our zero-tolerance stance on violence. We'll also be cracking down on anyone caught looting or causing destruction to private or public property.

"Inevitably, in situations like this, the criminal element will attempt to hijack the movement or use it as cover for other misdeeds. We saw plenty of that last night. It is unfortunate, but I will not strip away the civil rights of legitimate protestors because of a few bad apples.

"I realize that the occupation will come at a cost. I believe it is our duty to suffer alongside our young brothers and sisters, to stand with them in solidarity until the federal government addresses their complaint and makes them whole on the future that has been stolen from them."

"So I guess that means we're stuck here for a while." Lilith's voice sounded cheerless.

Shane thought hard. "We'll figure something out."

CHAPTER 7

So I returned, and considered all the oppressions that are done under the sun: and behold the tears of such as were oppressed, and they had no comforter; and on the side of their oppressors there was power; but they had no comforter.

Ecclesiastes 4:1

Late Sunday morning, Shane called Miguel. "Hey, buddy. How you guys holding up?"

"Watching the news. Staying inside. Not much else we can do. We ate at Jake's this morning, but the selection and the service left something to be desired."

"I think it's the same story all over town. You

guys should make sure you have food to get you through 'till tomorrow."

"Did you see the mayor's speech? I don't think it's going to get any better tomorrow. In fact, it might be worse. He basically said the protestors have permission to camp wherever they want."

"Yeah, I saw that. But we're getting out of here tomorrow. Once the city starts running out of food because delivery trucks can't get in, New York will look less like summer camp and more like an apocalyptic nightmare."

Miguel argued, "But it's their own fault!"

"This whole thing is their own fault. It's a failed socialist experiment. But that doesn't keep them from blaming it on capitalism. Not that the Republicans have turned down the excesses of easy money for their pet projects. Nor have they made any attempts to fix or scrap Social Security, but it's a product of progressivism."

"So what's the plan?"

"Derrick and Bridgette fly out of JFK tomorrow at 2:00 PM. I'm going to book flights for us out of here also. It might not be on the same plane as Derrick, but we'll leave the city together.

"Do you guys have black hoodies?"

Miguel responded, "I've got like a heather-gray one."

"Close enough. What about Casey?"

"I'm sure he has something like that."

"Good. I'm going to make cardboard signs that make us look like we're supporting the movement. We'll leave at first light in the morning. The Queensboro Bridge is only five blocks from here.

Hopefully, once we're across, we'll be able to get a cab to the airport.

"Obviously, you can't bring any luggage. Put anything of value on the bus, and we'll send someone to get it once the crisis abates."

Miguel sounded perturbed. "If it abates."

"Yeah. Sunrise is at 7:20. You guys be in the lobby here at 7:00 tomorrow morning."

"See you then." Miguel ended the call.

***

Early Monday morning, Shane pulled the batteries out of the small recording device he used to capture performances for his own personal library. Then, he took the batteries out of the camera Lilith used for taking live action shots to be used in marketing material and press releases.

"What are you doing?" She rolled over in the bed.

"Taking the batteries out of your camera."

"Why?"

"I'm going to put them in a sock. I can use it as a weapon if need be. Other than a couple of steak knives I managed to swipe from the restaurant yesterday, we don't have much in the self-defense department."

She sat up. "You're scaring me."

"I'm trying to keep you safe. I'm sure I don't have to remind you of the situation we're in."

"No." She pulled her hair out of her face. "What time is it?"

"5:30. We need to be ready to leave in one hour."

"You should have woken me up earlier. I can't get ready in an hour."

"You have plenty of time to take a shower and get dressed. No makeup today. You're supposed to look like a protestor, not a Hollywood starlet."

"They're protestors, not refugees. I'm sure the girls still wear makeup." Lilith stretched as she made her way to the shower.

"If you insist on wearing makeup, go easy on it." Yesterday's French bread was already getting stiff, but Shane used it to make sandwiches with the cold cuts he'd bought from the sub shop in the Plaza Food Hall.

Next, he started making signs on cardboard scavenged from the kitchen.

Lilith came out of the shower in record time. "You should cut the sleeves out of a black tee-shirt. You and Derrick can slip the sleeves over your heads and wear them around the bottom of your faces. Not only will it add to the civil-dissident look, but it will also keep me from having to explain why America's favorite country music stars are carrying signs that say *Occupy Everything*. Where there's trouble, there's always cameras. And you boys *will* be recognized."

"Good idea." Shane hated even acting like he was part of the movement.

The two of them finished getting ready. Shane looked around the room. "Do you have everything you need?"

Lilith looked at her suitcase still on the bed. "No. But it's all you'll let me take."

"We can buy new clothes, but if we fail to

convince these people that we're with them, we'll never make it across the bridge." He didn't like being so stern, but Stan was dead and Bobby was locked up. Everything had to go perfectly. "Let's get going."

Lilith frowned but followed him out the door with only her small backpack purse over her shoulder. Derrick and Bridgette's room was on the top floor. They took the elevator up.

Shane stood by their door and knocked.

"Just a second," Bridgette called from inside.

When she finally opened the door, she did not look like a protestor.

Shane shook his head.

"I tried to tell her." Derrick held his arms out as if helpless.

"You can't wear knee-high boots. Don't you have tennis shoes?" asked Shane.

"Just my gym shoes, but they're pink."

"Color doesn't matter as much as being able to run. That could be the difference in life or death."

Bridgette scowled. "I love these boots, and if I put them in my carry-on, I'll have to leave a bunch of stuff behind."

"You're not taking a carry-on."

"Shane, you can't tell me what I can and can't take. I've already been through this with Derrick."

"I'm sorry, it's not happening. You'll jeopardize all of our safety."

She turned to her husband. "Are you going to let him boss me around like that?"

Derrick sighed as if hating the situation. "Is it really that big of a deal, Shane?"

"It's that big of a deal. Do this my way or we can split up."

"We're not going to split up!" Lilith's voice got louder and higher.

"Lilith, don't fight me on this. Derrick and Bridgette will be flying back in cold storage next to Stan if they don't exercise some common sense in this situation. I love them both, but I can't make them do anything. You, on the other hand, are my responsibility, and we're doing this my way."

Bridgette began crying, relieving her of some of the excess mascara that needed to go anyway. "Fine, I change into my stupid gym shoes and leave my carry-on. Can I at least wash my face before we go?"

Shane nodded. "Sure, but you don't have time to reapply your makeup. Miguel and Casey are probably already waiting for us in the lobby. We have to go now."

An awkward silence ruled the moments while they waited for Bridgette to get ready. Derrick glanced up at Shane several times as if he wanted to apologize for the delay. Eventually, she emerged from the hotel room. Her face was pouty, but she'd complied with Shane's requests.

"Let's get moving. We don't want you guys to miss your flight." Shane led the way down the hall. "I had a hard enough time getting seats for all of us. Lilith and I have to go through Boston with a four-hour layover. Casey and Miguel have to go through Chicago. Their layover is three hours."

"Protests are popping up in both of those cites." Derrick stepped into the elevator.

Shane frowned. "Yeah, I saw."

They reached the lobby and Shane rushed to his bandmates. He handed a cardboard sign to each of them.

"Where's my bailout?" Casey read his sign aloud.

Miguel shook his head. "I can't believe it's come to this. I feel so dirty."

"Put your scarf around your face." Lilith pulled Miguel's scarf up over his mouth. "We don't want any cameras to recognize you feeling dirty."

"You, too." She pulled Casey's hood up over his head to obscure his face.

"We need to roll. Casey and Miguel's flight is at 12:30." Shane led the way.

Once out the door of the hotel, they'd entered the realm of the protestors. Shane scanned the area. All of the demonstrators around the Sherman Memorial were lethargic. They were bundled up with sleeping bags wrapped around them like capes. Some made coffee. A group of supporters brought a cardboard box filled with food and was handing it out to those who'd slept in the plaza around the statue.

He guided the march down East 59th Street seeing no other encampments along the way. They reached the ramp to the Queensboro Bridge quickly.

"I don't see any protestors," Derrick commented.

Lilith pointed ahead. "They'll be up ahead, under the flyover which provides a roof."

Shane maintained the pace knowing they were still a long way from JFK Airport. Shortly after ascending the ramp, the tents, foldable tables, and barrel fires came into view. "We'll slow down now.

Try to blend in. Smile and nod but try not to engage. Speak only if spoken to. Keep it short and polite."

Shane's group passed the first gathering of campers without so much as a glance. They appeared not to notice them at all. A couple of guys smiled at Lilith and Bridgette, but the four men in Shane's group seemed invisible to them. Once they passed the shelter of the flyover, the bridge was empty.

"Let's increase our stride until we run into more people." Shane broke into a slow jog.

The wind whipped across the East River and over the bridge.

"I've got to give them credit." Lilith pulled her hood tightly over her head. "I wouldn't want to be camping in this weather."

Shane moderated their speed when the protestors on the Queens' side of the bridge came into view. "Nice and leisurely. With any luck, we'll breeze right past these guys just like we did with the people on the other side."

One of the more militant demonstrators was near the end of the bridge, handing out flyers. He caught Shane as they were passing by. "Read this. We're trying to formalize a list of demands. The mayor's office is going to help us negotiate with the federal government. We've got their attention. We need to make something happen fast. If not, we may have to take our tactics up a notch. Nobody wants to still be sleeping out here in the cold come mid-January."

"Okay, we'll look it over, thanks." Shane offered a quick nod and a smile, then kept walking.

"Where are you guys going, anyway?"

"To find some breakfast. We'll pick up some extra for everyone if we can find anything affordable." Shane paused. "Any ideas?"

The militant with the flyers peered at him suspiciously. "There's a little market by the bridge. It'll be on the left. When you get to the bottom, circle back toward the river."

"Thanks. Want us to pick you up anything in particular?"

His glare softened. "Maybe a latte."

"Sugar?" Shane kept walking.

"Sure."

"Be right back." Shane waved and kept his party moving.

Once they were out of earshot, Miguel said, "If music doesn't work out for you, Shane, you can always get work in Hollywood."

"What would you do?" Casey asked Miguel.

"Be part of Shane's entourage. We'll let you drive the limo," Miguel joked.

Shane appreciated their attempt at keeping things light, but he was stressed. "You two take the first cab we find so you can make your flight. The rest of us will get the next one."

CHAPTER 8

He that hath knowledge spareth his words: and a man of understanding is of an excellent spirit. Even a fool, when he holdeth his peace, is counted wise: and he that shutteth his lips is esteemed a man of understanding.

Proverbs 17:27-28

Shane surveyed the streets for a taxi but saw none.
"There's one!" Casey whistled for the car turning off of Crescent Street.
"See you when we get home." Derrick waved.
Miguel and Casey threw a hand in the air and took off running after the yellow vehicle which

soon stopped for them.

The rest of the group continued their easterly travel. Two blocks later, Shane spotted a second cab. He whistled loudly and hailed the taxi. Shane tossed his cardboard sign onto the side of the street and opened the door for Lilith. Derrick and Bridgette got into the rear of the vehicle. Shane rode up front with the driver. "JFK, please. They're going to American first, then you can drop us at Jet Blue."

The cabbie looked Shane over. "You left your signs."

"That was just a ruse," Bridgette said. "To get us over the bridge."

He glanced up to his rearview mirror as he set the meter. "What, you don't believe in the occupation?"

Shane could hear the disapproving undertones in the driver's voice. "It's not that we don't support the movement, but we need to get home, so we can be more effective."

"Where's home?" asked the driver who sounded like a Queens native.

"Nashville," Derrick answered.

"Nashville." The cab driver sounded condescending in the way he repeated it back.

Shane hoped no one would engage. Unfortunately, that's not how it worked out.

"Why? What's wrong with Nashville?" Bridgette sounded offended.

"Oh, nothing. I just haven't heard anything about anyone demonstrating there."

"You're going on about your business," Lilith

added. "I don't see you out there with a sign."

"Let's just enjoy a nice quiet ride to the airport," Shane interjected.

"Quiet ride to the airport he says. Tah!" The cabbie scowled. He looked up at the rearview. "I'll have you know that I took donuts and coffee to this side of the Queensboro Bridge *and* to the entrance of the Mid-Town Tunnel before I started my shift this morning. Paid for it out of my own pocket."

No one responded to his statement. Shane watched the man out of the corner of his eye. The taxi driver was stewing in resentment of his passengers. When he reached the bottom of the Queens Boulevard Overpass, he made a sharp U-turn.

"What are you doing?" Shane asked.

"What does it look like I'm doing? I'm turning around. I'm going to take you back to the bridge. Then, after you explain how you snuck across to the people out there fighting for what they believe in, you can find another taxi to take you to JFK."

"You can't do that!" Shane exclaimed.

"It's my cab, my city, and my decision. Ain't no cowpoke gonna come up here and tell me what I can and can't do."

"No, I mean you can't take us back. Some of these protestors are violent. They'll kill us if you tell them that!" Shane's heart pounded.

"Shoulda thought of that earlier," the cabbie smirked.

"Sir, please. I'm very sorry if we offended you, but we can't go back to the bridge." Shane continued trying to reason with the man.

"Too late for that. You shoulda stayed down in hillbilly country."

Shane's mouth went dry thinking about the last encounter which had cost Stan his life and Bobby his freedom. He gently put his hand in the pocket of his hoodie and took hold of the sock filled with batteries. The cab stopped at the 28th Street traffic light. Shane knew he had only a few blocks before they'd be back to the bridge. He had to act now.

Shane slung the sock filled with batteries around and came down hard on the nose of the driver.

Blood spurted out and the taxi driver cried out in shock. "Ahhh! What did you do that for?" He covered his nose with both hands.

Shane swung again, this time aiming for the side of the man's head. BOP! The weighted sock slapped his temple and the man's eyes closed. Shane grabbed the shifter and put the car in park before it began to roll.

"What are you doing?" Bridgette screamed.

Shane pulled the man's body toward the passenger's seat and simultaneously crawled over him. "Trying to stay alive. Give me a hand!"

Derrick reached over the seat and assisted getting the driver out of the way so Shane could take the wheel. Shane rushed to get into position and threw the shifter in gear. He punched the gas pedal and drove over the pedestrian walkway onto Queens Plaza. "Derrick, take off your belt and put it around this guy's neck. If he comes to, keep the pressure on it. The instant he starts talking or acting belligerent, choke him out."

"He's not dead?" Lilith sounded upset.

Shane glanced over, only for a second. "I hope not." Shane weaved through the streets trying to make his way back toward the airport. "Lilith, I need you to pull up a map and get me some directions."

"We're still going to the airport?" she asked.

"Unless someone has a better plan." Shane held his breath as he drove past an NYPD patrol car.

"What about the driver? What are we going to do with him?" Derrick draped his belt over the front seat and fished it around the cabbie's throat.

Hating the situation, Shane gritted his teeth. "Tie him up, I guess."

"With what?" asked Lilith.

Shane glanced over at the driver's feet. "His shoe strings. We'll go to long-term parking, tie him up, and put him in the trunk. Someone will find him eventually."

"I hope they find him after we're in the air." Derrick took up the slack in the belt.

"Me, too." Shane listened to Lilith's directions and navigated toward the airport.

Minutes later, the driver began to groan.

"Keep that belt tight, Derrick!" Shane focused on his driving.

"Why did you do that?" asked the aching cabbie.

"You gave me no choice. I was faced with being fed to the wolves and taking on an angry mob of a hundred, or I could take you out. What would you have done?"

"Listen, guy. I've got a daughter. Her wedding is in two weeks. I just want to walk her down the aisle."

"You still might get the chance to do that. But I'd recommend that you conduct yourself very circumspectly. Tell me something, if we let you live, are you going to blow the whistle as soon as somebody finds you? Obviously, you know where we're going. If the authorities have the resources to look into it, I'm sure they'd eventually catch up to us."

"No, I swear on my life."

Shane still wore his face mask as did Derrick, but the man had seen the girls' faces. "I want to believe you, but I'm not in the habit of taking strangers at their word. Especially after they've tried to have me killed."

"What are you talking about? I didn't try to kill anybody!"

"That mob very well may have killed all four of us. You knew that when you turned the car around."

"I never meant nothing like that. Please!"

Shane glanced up at the rearview. "Baby, reach over and get this guy's wallet out of his pants."

Lilith did so.

"Is his license in there?"

"Yeah." Her voice sounded nervous.

"Does it have his address?"

"Yes."

Shane turned to the driver. "I'm going to hang on to your wallet. I'll memorize your address. If we have any trouble, any whatsoever, you won't make it to that wedding. That's if there's a wedding at all. Do you understand me?"

"Yes. You won't have any trouble on my account. Believe me!" The man's voice quaked with fear.

They pulled into the long-term parking lot. Shane cut the engine, wiped the fingerprints from the steering wheel with the sleeve of his hoodie and removed the driver's shoes. He pulled out the man's shoelaces and proceeded to bind the cabbie's hands. Shane looked back at Derrick. "Open the door for him so he can get out."

Shane walked around and opened the trunk. He and Derrick put the man inside, then tied his feet. "If I hear any yelling or banging on the trunk, your next family gathering will be a funeral, not a wedding. Their flight is soon, but mine's not for a couple of hours. I'm going to hang around out here and make sure you behave. Do you understand me?" Shane used the steak knife taken from the hotel to cut off the emergency trunk release handle.

The man nodded in trepidation. "I understand."

"Nothing. Not a peep. If I open this trunk, it's all over for you." Shane pointed the steak knife at the driver's neck and closed the trunk.

Shane walked around the vehicle and wiped all the door handles for prints. Then, he held his finger over his mouth to signal for the others to be quiet and led them to the airport.

Once out of earshot, Lilith asked, "Are we going to take the shuttle?"

"No, they probably have cameras. We'll be walking by plenty of those when we get to the concourse. We don't want to make it any easier for them to find us. Everyone, ditch your hoodies before we walk into the airport."

"Are you going to keep that poor guy's wallet?"

Bridgette asked.

Shane would be happy when he no longer had to deal with Bridgette. She'd made a difficult situation even more arduous at every possible opportunity. He glanced at his watch. She and Derrick had only another hour until their flight. "That *poor guy* tried to kill you, Bridgette. I'm sure that even he appreciates the fact that he's getting off very easy here." Shane took the cash out of the wallet, wiped it for prints, and tossed it in the next available trash can.

The walk to the airport entrance was about three miles. Oddly enough, Shane and his companions weren't the only pedestrians. Several other young people were milling around the perimeter roads.

A young girl jogged up to Lilith. "Hey, do you know where we're supposed to be going?"

"For?" Lilith looked at the girl like she was nuts.

"Occupy JFK. I got a tweet saying we were going to shut down the airport today. Supposedly everyone is going to stand on the tarmac, but I don't have any idea how to get over there."

Shane quickly took control of the conversation. "I saw a sign for the Port Authority Police Department. It's up ahead. We were going to try to cut through there."

"Right in front of the cops?" The girl seemed surprised.

"Yeah." Shane lifted his shoulders. "I guess we'll see if Mayor Greenwell really has our backs with this thing."

"Yeah." The girl waved and jogged back to her friends. "I guess so."

"Let's hope we can get in the air before they shut down the airport." Shane quickened his stride toward the airport entrance.

Shane and Lilith parted ways with Derrick and Bridgette when they reached the American Airlines terminal.

"See you when we get home." Derrick waved.

"Have a good flight," said Shane.

CHAPTER 9

When one gets in bed with government, one must expect the diseases it spreads.

Ron Paul

Shane and Lilith paced around outside the terminal rather than spend time inside the airport where cameras surveilled every inch and every second. Shane watched a plane take off and circle overhead. He glanced at the clock on his phone. "That was probably Derrick and Bridgette. At least we know they made it out."

"When are we going inside? I'm freezing out here." Lilith rubbed her arms.

"The plane will probably start boarding in an hour. We should go ahead and check in." Shane stuffed his black hoodie into the trash can on the way into the Jet Blue concourse. He emptied his pockets of the black shirt sleeve that he'd used for a face mask, the sock filled with batteries, and the steak knife from the hotel, discarding them all in like manner.

The two of them walked to the counter and presented their IDs. The middle-aged female attendant took them and typed in some information on her computer. Her forehead wrinkled while she looked at the screen.

Shane felt anxious. He wondered if the cabbie had gotten out, called the police and described Shane and the others. The woman kept typing, as if she were working on a short story which was overdue. Her face did not lighten. Shane determined that if she walked away from the counter to make a phone call, he and Lilith would make a run for it. If they'd been identified, he'd contact an attorney and turn himself in at another location. He did not want to be hauled off to Riker's Island while a bond was being negotiated, especially in the midst of the chaos happening in New York City.

"Is everything okay?" Shane hoped his voice didn't sound as nervous as he felt.

The woman held up a finger, signaling that she did not want to be disturbed. The printer began noisily clacking and clicking, slowly feeding a document into the woman's hand. Finally, she looked up, jerked the document from the printer with a controlled rip and handed it to Shane. "Here are your boarding passes. Don't you have luggage?" She peered at him suspiciously, as if he might be a terrorist or drug mule.

"No." He saw no reason to get into the details if it could be avoided.

"Okay." She offered a contrived smile. "Enjoy your flight."

"Thank you." Shane handed Lilith her boarding pass and led the way to the security checkpoint. He felt relieved that they'd had no problems at check-in, but still felt apprehensive about proceeding through TSA.

He and Lilith removed their shoes, emptied their pockets, and prepared to receive standardized doses of radiation from the body scanner in hopes of avoiding further degradation via an invasive pat down. He watched two young male agents hurry over to watch the scanner as Lilith walked through, knowing exactly what they were doing. Still, having her electronic nakedness gawked at by the underqualified perverts seemed preferable to watching some depraved TSA employee running her hands over his fiancé's body and groping her between the legs.

He kept his displeasure about the situation to himself and walked through. They collected their belongings, put their shoes back on and continued toward the gate.

"Can we stop at the bar? I need a drink."

"We're flying first class. You can get a drink once we board."

"I need a drink now. I don't even want to talk about what we've been through since we left the hotel this morning."

"I know, baby. But let's wait."

"Why? What difference does it make?"

"We need to keep our wits about us. Just in case."

"In case of what?"

"In case we see the police running toward us. In case the airport gets closed down by protestors. I'm sure I'm not even thinking of all the things that could go wrong right now." Shane regularly looked to his left and right, scanning for danger. "How about we get something to eat?"

"Like what?"

He pointed to the food court. "Cheeburger Cheeburger or they've got a place for Phillies, Dunkin Donuts."

"I guess I'll take a burger."

He led the way to the counter. "Fries?"

"And a shake." She held his hand while they waited.

As they ate, Shane glanced back and forth from the departure time display board to the clock on his phone, paying little attention to Lilith or his food.

She reached across the table and put her hand on his. "It's okay. You can relax now. We made it."

He forced a smile and tried to let go of the uneasy feeling. "You're right. So, what are you going to do when we get home?"

"We never got to properly celebrate our engagement. We're going out on the town. Then, it's right back to work. You've got a tour starting in three weeks."

Shane looked down at his French fries. It wouldn't seem right to be out partying with Stan dead and Bobby still locked up. But, he knew Lilith had been robbed of her chance to toast their betrothal. "Sure. We'll make a big time of it."

He imagined being in his own house, his own bed, far away from the troubles and turmoil of New York. He felt the tension melt from his neck and back, allowed his arms and face to soften. Shane took in a slow even breath. He looked up at the departure board once more and the tension rushed back in. His legs stiffened, knees, elbows, and jaw braced, as if for a punch from a prize fighter. His nostrils flared.

"Shane? Are you alright?" Lilith turned to see what he was looking at.

"Delayed. All the departure times are flipping. Every flight on the board. Delayed, delayed, delayed."

"Don't jump to conclusions," she said.

"Are you finished eating?"

"Yes."

"Then let's get going."

"Where?"

"I'm going to ask the desk agent what's going on." He grabbed her hand and tugged her to the nearest service counter.

"Excuse me, Miss?"

The agent looked annoyed. "Yes?"

"Do you know what caused the delays?"

She let out an exhale of exasperation. "Evidently, unauthorized people are on the runway."

"All the runways?"

"No. Just 4L-22R."

"Planes can't take off on the other runways?"

"Not until the situation is under control."

"Thank you." Shane led Lilith toward the exit.

"What are we doing?" she asked.

"We've got to get a cab while we still can."

"They might have it cleared up in a few minutes."

"You heard Greenwell. He's backing this movement. So is New York's governor. The demonstrators have carte blanche to do whatever they want. If we waste any time, everyone in the airport will be fighting for a taxi, and we'll be stuck again."

"Where will we go?"

"Anywhere away from here." Shane moved as fast as possible without breaking into a full sprint.

Once outside, Shane took the first taxi he saw. He held the door for Lilith then got inside.

"Where to?" The driver had a thick Indian accent.

"Are any of the bridges out of New York open?"

"Probably is still open 278 out of Staten Island. If not, for sure is open Outerbridge."

"Good. Let's go there."

"Okay." The cabbie set his meter and began driving away from the terminal. "Then where you go?"

"Away from the city." Shane had nowhere to go, but he was in a hurry to get there.

"Away how far?"

"Until we see cows."

The cabbie laughed. "I don't know where is cow."

Shane realized how ridiculous his request must sound to someone confined to an asphalt jungle for months on end. "I'll settle for trees and grass."

"And a hotel," Lilith added. "I'm not standing around outside anymore today."

Shane had no idea what he'd do next, so a place to regroup and come up with a game plan would probably be best. "And a hotel," he echoed.

"Maybe Bridgewater, New Jersey. Is away from the city. They have grass and tree and hotel."

"Is it far?"

"Normally, like one hour. But a lot of traffic because of the protest. Could be couple hours just to get out of New York. Don't worry. I take you there. Is good place. You like very much."

"Is it somewhere you go often?" Lilith asked curiously.

Shane squeezed her hand as a reminder of what too much conversation with cabbies had gotten them early that day.

The driver smiled and patted his turban. "Yes. A lot of Sikh. I have uncle over there."

The drive took more than three hours, but Shane was happy to be out. They checked into a hotel room and ordered a pizza for dinner.

CHAPTER 10

It is well enough that people of the nation do not understand our banking and monetary system, for if they did, I believe there would be a revolution before tomorrow morning.

Henry Ford

Early Tuesday morning, Shane checked his phone. "The rental car is downstairs. Let's go."

"Sure, just let me grab my things." Lilith sounded sardonic as she walked into the hallway. "Oh, that's right, I don't have any things to grab."

He gave an unimpressed smile at her cynical humor and closed the door behind them.

Once outside, Shane met the man delivering the

vehicle, a Jeep Cherokee.

The employee gave him a clipboard. "If you'll just sign here, initial here, and here, you'll be good to go, Mr. Black."

"Sure." Shane filled in the appropriate spaces with the pen.

"They didn't have a real SUV?" Lilith looked over his shoulder while he completed the form.

"They had a Yukon, but it was double the price. Big gas mileage difference as well. At $10 a gallon, it adds up."

She rolled her eyes. "I can't believe you're counting pennies over all this."

Shane handed the clipboard back to the man. "Thanks."

"We'll pick up the car at your address in Nashville on Thursday morning. Just give us a call if you need to keep it longer." The man got into another car which would take him back to the office. "Drive safe."

"I will." Shane got in and started the engine. He waited for Lilith to put her seat belt on before putting the vehicle into gear.

"Road trip," she said unenthusiastically. "I'll just think of it as a warm up for the tour."

Shane pulled out of the lot and headed toward the highway. "If things don't get resolved soon, there won't be a tour."

"There will be a tour. Otherwise, we'll have our own personal financial crisis."

"Maybe we should start scaling back our spending."

"I don't spend a lot of money."

Dysphoria

"We could get by on less."

"If Backwoods can't get by, then everyone else in the music industry is going to starve to death. I don't think it's all that bad yet. We had a bad experience in New York is all. That, coupled with your dad's post-apocalyptic worldview has you a little shaken up. We'll get home, relax for a few days, and you'll be fine."

Once on the highway, Shane called Barry Rothstein.

"Shane," the man answered over the speakerphone. "Still nothing about Bobby."

"The courts are open today, right?"

"Yes, but they're clogged up after a holiday weekend anyway. In addition to all of that, people can't get to work. It's gridlock up there because of the protests. Our guy is working on it. He has a teleconference with the ADA this afternoon. Once that happens, the recommendations will go to the judge, then he'll either set bond or drop the charges."

"He'll talk to the judge today?"

"Probably be more like tomorrow. But we've put money on Bobby's commissary account. He'll be okay until we can get him out."

"Okay, Barry, but this has to be your priority."

"It is, trust me."

Shane hated when lawyers said *trust me*. "Thanks, let me know when you hear something." He ended the call and turned on the radio to distract himself from the situation with Bobby. The first station he reached was covering the riots.

A female reporter elaborated on the Occupy movement. "Demonstrators are now in every major metropolitan area to protest what they see as a bad deal. With gas nearing the ten-dollar-mark for the first time in history, and grocery prices more than doubling in many instances, it's understandable why people are feeling abandoned by their governments. The mayors of Oakland, Philadelphia, Austin, Chicago, Seattle, and Boulder, have all joined Mayor Greenwell of New York in what he has termed Occupy City Hall. All have pledged not to interfere with the protestors' rights to voice their grievances over the economic unfairness. They've said they'll do everything they can to support and protect the demonstrators, but have asked that violence not be part of the program.

"President Donovan is expected to address the country this evening. His office stated that he'll talk about the protests and lay out a plan which will alleviate some of the negative effects of the bailout.

"We have a special guest on the line to help us understand a little bit about how things have gotten so out of control. Dr. William Galloway is an Economics Professor at Cornell University. Dr. Galloway, thank you for making time for us today. Can you explain what happened?"

"Yes, Sharon, thanks for having me. I'll probably be reprimanded for what I'm about to say because it's not the official line in academia, but what happened is we dumbed down our population. Essentially, we've turned our country into a nation of low-information voters."

"Pardon me, Dr. Galloway, but I thought we

were going to talk about economics. What you're saying sounds offensive."

"Please don't be offended, I'm not blaming the public. And we most certainly are talking about economics. But through the public education system, our population has not been given the proper tools to make informed choices about who they put in charge. That's the root cause. We can blame it on the politicians, but we're the ones who put them in office.

"The way I see it, the dollar is in the throes of death. This problem has been unsolvable for well over a decade. It was already too late when we hit the housing crisis back in '08 and '09. The things we had to do to keep the ship afloat were beyond unsustainable. We made the big banks bigger. We doubled the money supply, which is the equivalent of sawing off a tree branch that you're sitting on. And here we are, still sawing away at that branch.

"We've never been able to normalize interest rates because to do so would have pushed us over the edge that much faster. So, the Fed doesn't have the interest rate mechanism to help right the ship through this storm. Not that it would have any effect this time around anyway. We're talking about lowering the jib to offset the effects of a hundred-foot rogue wave.

"My peers have lots of free time on their hands and one of the things we like to do with that time is to develop what we consider pithy allegories for the complex functions of markets and currency. One such allegory is the black swan, which represents rare economic anomalies that can trigger systemic upheaval. But in our endeavor to be overly succinct, we often fail to grasp the full scope of our own analogies. Black swans are a separate species, not a white swan that happened to get an atypical roll of the genetic dice. As such, they live in groups called a lamentation, which takes our example one step deeper. So, while it may be uncommon to see a black swan if you do happen to witness such a creature, you're very likely to view several of them. It's even quite possible that you'll behold an entire lamentation of black swans."

The woman sounded perplexed by the dissertation. "Are you saying we are experiencing a lamentation of black swans?"

"It sounds more ominous to hear you say it, but yes. Think back with me to the Great Depression. We had not only a stock market crash but the decade that followed also saw the worst drought in American history.

"Then in the housing crisis, we saw not only poor lending standards fuel a housing bubble, but we also saw corruption on a grand scale where banks would go to their buddies to get subprime debt rated as triple-A so they could fetch a premium price for financial products they knew to be garbage. Given, those components are more closely related than a market downturn and a drought, but they exacerbated one another in the same way. In each of these instances, we saw two black swans together.

"This time, a lamentation. We have the burgeoning national debt, which neither party has wanted to address for decades. We have the Social

Security time bomb, which has finally exploded. The public and private pension systems have collapsed. The working man had already been reduced to near-poverty standards by inflation, and now he's been kicked off the ladder altogether. People can't even get by; that inevitably results in civil unrest.

"I mentioned the interest rate problem earlier. These unprecedented rates have forced fund managers and people nearing retirement to reach for the stars in terms of trying to eke out gains for their portfolios. The people who could afford it the least have been forced to take on unheard-of financial risk.

"We have a fiat currency system which has worn out its welcome on the world stage and is being shoved into retirement.

"All of these issues are like cogs in a machine designed to drag us under and bury us in the abyss. Fixing any single problem, assuming any of them could be fixed, would do very little to address the overall picture.

"In short, we had a good run, but the party is over. It's time to go home."

The woman said, "I'm not sure I follow you. What do you mean go home? Where's home?"

The professor laughed. "Good question. For the country, we'll be swept into the dust bin of history, just as the Roman Empire was, and all the empires that came before it. Personally, a bomb shelter would probably be your best bet, preferably one that is well stocked with food and ammo. Because what we're about to experience is going to be chaos never before imagined by the human mind. Perhaps the only redeeming quality of our future is that it's going to be interesting. I just hope they can manage to keep the power on so we can watch it on television."

The woman seemed eager to wrap up the interview. "Dr. Galloway, I don't think we were expecting such a dire outlook from you, but thank you for your time."

"Dire?" laughed the professor. "Honey, I'm sugarcoating it. I intentionally glossed over the killing, prostitution, cannibalism, and all the other things people do to survive when empires fail and currencies expire. As I said, you cannot fathom what is coming next."

Lilith pushed the power button and turned off the radio. "Wow! I never thought I'd say this, but that guy is even more paranoid than your dad. I can't believe they let somebody like that teach at a college. He's crazy."

"Unless he's right."

She looked at Shane as if he were joking. "You can't be serious. You're not buying into the whole end-of-civilization rant we just heard, are you?"

Shane wasn't sure what was going on, but he wasn't as quick to dismiss his father's concerns as he'd been a week ago.

CHAPTER 11

Upon the land of my people shall come up thorns and briers; yea, upon all the houses of joy in the joyous city: because the palaces shall be forsaken; the multitude of the city shall be left; the forts and towers shall be for dens for ever, a joy of wild asses, a pasture of flocks.

Isaiah 32:13-14

Shane glanced down at his fuel gauge, then to the range indicator on the driver information display. "We need to stop for gas soon."

"Good. I want to get something to eat." Lilith pointed at the sign on the side of the road. "Roanoke should have something besides fast food or Cracker Barrel."

Shane took the next exit and pulled up to the gas station. "Out of gas?" He read the hand-written sign aloud.

Lilith reapplied her lipstick and checked her hair in the visor mirror. "There's an Exxon across the street and a Shell next door to it."

Shane navigated around the pumps and crossed over the road to the next service station. "Look at that. They're out also."

"That's insane. Check the Shell station."

Shane quickly whipped the Jeep back onto the road and turned off once more. "No way! Out of gas. I'm going to ask this guy what's going on." Shane cut the engine and exited the vehicle.

"I'm coming with you." Lilith tagged along close behind.

Shane opened the door. "Hey."

"Howdy," replied the attendant, an older man with a well-trimmed beard.

"Is there a fuel shortage or something I don't know about? Did you and the other stations not get deliveries today?"

"We got 'em, but we sold out. The BP was out by 11:00 this morning. We tapped out shortly after lunch, and Exxon ran dry right about the time we did."

Lilith wrinkled her forehead. "Why would people be in a rush to pay $10 for gas?"

"Because they think it might be $12 tomorrow, I reckon," said the attendant.

"Do you think we'll find gas if we drive into Roanoke?" Shane inquired.

"Nope. Most of the stations in town ran out early this morning. It was mostly folks from town who drove out here and bought everything we had."

"Where's the closest place I'd be able to find gas?" Shane asked.

"Beats me." The man looked at his watch. "If I knew, they'd probably be empty, too, because I'd have been sending people there for three hours by now."

Shane looked around at the shelves which were sparsely stocked. "Do you have any gas cans?" He figured if they did find gas, he should get a little extra to make sure it would be enough to get them home.

"Sold out early this morning."

Shane pressed his lips together tightly in disappointment. Obviously, the idea had hit someone else much sooner. "Okay, thanks."

The attendant waived. "It ain't none of my business what you do, but if you want some friendly advice, I'd be glad to give it."

Shane turned on his way out the door. "Sure, please."

"Lots of folks are coming in off the highway. Some of them have been looking for gas for a hundred miles or more. If you don't have enough fuel to get you home, you should start looking for a hotel. They'll be filling up soon. Won't be no rooms neither."

"Okay, thanks. I appreciate the tip." Shane waved.

"Hang on a second."

Shane turned. "Yes?"

"Ain't you the fella who plays guitar for Backwoods?"

"Yes, sir." Shane certainly didn't feel like being a celebrity at the moment, but the man had given him some very valuable advice.

"Is that the little gal you got engaged to on New Year's?"

Lilith waved with an insincere smile. "I'm *the little gal.*"

"Well, I'll be doggone." The man seemed elated to have country music royalty in his filling station. "Congratulations. Sorry them folks up in New York sorta ruined it for you."

"They didn't ruin anything. We were just happy to be together." Shane's smile was more genuine. "Any idea what time you'll have more gas?"

"Truck usually comes in about 5:00 AM. You might want to be here about 4:30 if you don't want to get stuck in a line."

Shane hated the thought of getting up that early. "Thank you very much. Have a good evening."

Once they were outside, Lilith asked, "So we're staying here?"

He opened the door for her. "The information display says we can go about twenty-five miles, so yeah, we're staying here." Shane returned to the driver's seat and started the engine.

"I'm not staying at Days Inn, so don't even try there." She buckled her seat belt and crossed her arms.

"Nothing around here is probably going to be what you're used to. We're looking for a better option than sleeping in the vehicle. It's going to get cold tonight, and we have no gear." Shane turned in the opposite direction of the Days Inn. "Looks like you can choose between Hampton and Country Inn."

"There's a Fairfield. Try there first."

Shane pulled up behind another car at the front door of the entrance. "I'll see if they have anything. Stay with the car."

No sooner had he closed the door than the driver of the vehicle in front of him came out shaking his head. "Full."

"Thanks." Shane returned to the vehicle and drove to the Hampton. He went inside only to learn that they also had no vacancies.

He crossed his fingers as he walked into the lobby of the Country Inn. He approached the young woman at the front desk. "Do you have any rooms available?"

"Sorry, we're booked."

"Any suggestions?"

"Did you try the Days Inn? It's a bigger hotel. They might have a few rooms left."

"Anything else?" He didn't want to listen to Lilith complaining all night.

"The new hotel right behind the Fairfield. It's off the main road, so I think people don't see it."

"Perfect. Thank you." Shane moved with a sense of urgency back to the car.

"Nothing?"

"No." He pulled out of the parking lot with haste.

"Are you going back to Days Inn?" Lilith looked worried. "I'm not trying to be a princess or anything, but I can't sleep anywhere that feels dirty."

"I know, baby. We've still got one more option." Shane turned off the main road, up the side road and into the parking lot of a newer hotel.

"It's a Hilton property. Must be their new economy line." Lilith looked around. "The lot isn't completely full. Looks promising."

She followed him inside. Shane approached the desk. "Hi, do you have any rooms available?"

The girl looked up from her computer. "I do, but our complimentary breakfast is not going to be fully stocked in the morning. We've had some issues with our supplier."

"I don't care about breakfast." Shane took out his ID and credit card.

"Additionally, we've had to adjust our rates, so if you saw a price on the internet, it might not reflect the adjustments."

"No problem." Shane slid his driver's license to the girl.

She seemed hesitant to take it. "It's $209 per night before tax, sir." She looked as if she were expecting an outburst.

Shane figured other travelers had already unleashed their fury on the poor girl. "That sounds great. We were paying over $1,000 a night for a junior suite at the Plaza in New York. Plus, it was essentially in the middle of a war zone, so this sounds like a bargain."

"Yes, sir." She appeared to be put at ease by his light-hearted comment and began entering his information into the computer.

Lilith leaned against the counter. "Are there any shops nearby? Like clothing boutiques?"

"Downtown has lots of shops." The girl continued to work diligently.

"How far is that?" asked Shane.

"About 8 miles."

"16 miles round trip. I don't want to risk it." Shane took her hand.

Lilith pulled away. "I've been wearing the same clothes for two days."

"Do any stores around here sell clothes?"

"Gander Mountain is right next door."

Lilith shook her head. "I'm not wearing camouflage pants and a duck hunting vest."

"They might have sweats or something." Shane inserted his credit card into the reader. "They sell camping and hiking gear. We should at least be able to find clean socks."

"Okay. I'll go for the clean socks." Lilith turned her attention to the girl. "What's good to eat around here?"

"I like the Mexican restaurant up the road. We also have a good seafood place on Williamson Road."

"Which is closer?" asked Shane.

"Mexican. It's next to the Country Inn."

"Mexican it is, then. We must have driven right past it." He took the key card from the girl. "Thank you for your help."

"Can we go to the camping store first? I'd like to take a shower and put on some clean clothes before we go eat."

"Sure." Shane led the way outside and across the

lot.

Once inside, Lilith took a cart. "Look, Under Armor leggings and compression shirts. These will work. Here's a hoodie. I just need a tee-shirt and some socks, and I'm good to go."

After Lilith had collected her necessities, Shane led the way to the men's department. He found a pair of jeans, some socks, and two plaid, flannel shirts. "Okay, let's go get cleaned up so we can eat."

On the way to the register, Shane paused near the camping gear. "We should get a pack so we're not hauling our dirty clothes home in a plastic bag. And look at this." He held up a canister of bear repellant.

"The hotel looked pretty clean. I'd be surprised if we see bugs, much less bears." Lilith pushed the cart down the aisle.

"I'm thinking in case we run into trouble when we get back to Nashville."

"You have a safe full of guns in Nashville."

"Yeah, but we have to get to the safe for them to do us any good." Shane put the bear spray in the cart.

"Here's some camping food. Maybe I'll get a few pouches of that as well."

"Camping food? I thought we were going to get Mexican?" Lilith sounded perturbed.

"In case things get worse."

Her voice got louder and higher pitched. "I thought we were supposed to be saving money. Why are you buying all of this junk like you think the world is imploding?"

"Lilith, we barely escaped New York with our

lives. Stan wasn't so lucky. Bobby is still there, locked up on Riker's Island. We had to abduct a taxi driver, stuff him in the trunk, and threaten his family. The airport was taken over by protestors. You can't keep plunging your head deeper and deeper into the sand, pretending nothing is wrong. From everything I'm seeing, the world may very well be imploding."

Her lip began to quiver. She seemed to be holding back as she tightened her jaw. Lilith turned her head away from Shane, but he could see the tears welling up in her eyes. Her face further contorted in emotion, then she broke down into loud sobs.

He pulled her close to comfort her. "Shhhh. It's going to be okay. We'll get through this, but we can't be naive about what is going on around us."

She sobbed, "I know. I just don't want this to be happening to us."

"Me neither, baby. But it's out of our hands. All we can do is try to get through it."

CHAPTER 12

We have made lies our refuge, and under falsehood have we hid ourselves.

Isaiah 28:15b

Tuesday evening after dinner, Shane pulled his boots off and reclined on the hotel bed.

Lilith crawled up next to him and offered him a sip from her Styrofoam to-go cup. "Want some?"

He grabbed the remote. "No. I have to get up at 4:00 AM to buy gas. I can't believe you got a margarita to go."

"It was either this or beer from the service station." She sucked on the straw. "After the past few days, I deserve a drink."

"You had two already at the restaurant."

"So?"

Shane's phone rang. "Hey, Dad."

"Son, how are y'all doing?"

"Stuck in Roanoke." Shane offered a sanitized version of their escape from New York, glossing over the more harrowing events.

Paul Black replied, "You and Lilith should come on home. We're closer than Nashville."

"Not that much closer."

"I've got fuel. I could come to get you."

"Thanks, Dad, but we'll be fine. Besides, we had to leave all our stuff in New York. Lilith doesn't even have clothes. We had to go buy stuff from Gander Mountain to have something clean to put on. The president is coming on in a few minutes. Supposedly they have a plan to get things back under control."

Paul chortled. "Yeah, they've always got a plan. Their high-minded ideas are what got us in this mess. The best thing the president could do right now is to stay in bed, because every morning when he gets up, he manages to sink us deeper in the hole than we were the day before. But I sound like a broken record. You know how I feel about all of it.

"My offer still stands. When things get bad enough, you and Lilith come on home. Don't expect anything out of the government. They're out of options. All they can do at this point is to keep printing more money until no one will take it. It's like fighting a forest fire with gasoline."

Shane considered his father's proposal. If it were only him, he'd go home in a heartbeat. But having Lilith and his parents together could prove to be more complicated than getting out of Manhattan. "Thanks, Dad. Lilith and I really do appreciate the invitation."

"Take care. We love you."

"I love you, too, Dad. Tell Mom I miss her." Shane ended the call.

"Still begging you to come home?" Lilith sipped her margarita.

"Yeah. He offered to come pick us up." Shane clicked on the television to scenes of riots and fires in Oakland filmed from a helicopter.

"No way! I'd rather parachute into the middle of that." Lilith pointed with the straw of her carry-out libation toward the chaos on the screen.

Shane watched the disorder in silence, hoping her flippant aspiration wouldn't be fulfilled. His phone buzzed. It was a text from Miguel. *Where R U?*

Shane briefly gave an account of their trip so far. He inquired via text, *Any protests in Nashville?*

Lilith leaned over to look on while Shane read the text. *Don't come through Nashville. Take 840 south and come up through Pasquo.*

Shane typed away at his keyboard. *Gas is tight. That's an extra 70 miles.*

He read Miguel's reply aloud. "Do what you want. Belle Meade is okay right now, but protestors are blocking all the main roads around Nashville."

Shane opened his calculator app and quickly did the math for the second part of their journey. "I'd need about another three gallons if I follow Miguel's recommendation."

"Can't we stop after about 100 miles and refuel?" asked Lilith.

"Maybe, but I'd rather have some extra fuel than take the gamble." Shane stuck his feet in his boots. "I'll be back. I'm going to see if I can find some gallon jugs of water."

"Get me some beer while you're out."

"I thought you didn't like beer."

"I've had two margaritas. I'm feeling a little less picky. Something imported though. And not Heineken or Corona. They're not considered imported in Germany or Mexico."

"Wouldn't that be true of all beers and their countries of origin?"

"Imported was the wrong word. See if they have any microbrews. If not, get Sam Adams."

Shane put his sweater on. "Premium was the word you were looking for."

"They kinda throw that term around a lot. It doesn't mean what it used to. Expensive, I think that's the adjective I was in search of."

Shane pulled the door closed behind him and muttered, "Isn't it always?" He hurried to the Jeep wanting to get back to the room before the president's address began. Shane drove to the BP which had the larger mini-mart of the three local filling stations.

Once inside, he noticed the same sparsely stocked shelves like those in the Shell station across the street. He took the last three gallons of water to the register. "Any idea what time your gas truck will be in?"

"I'm not sure. The manager said this thing with

OPEC could limit our availability. Corporate is prioritizing which stations will get gas first if there's a shortage."

"OPEC? What thing?"

The young man working the counter lifted his shoulders. "I don't know. Something about they don't want our money."

"As in they're not accepting dollars anymore?" Shane took out his credit card to pay for the water.

"That sounds right. I'm not real up on all the details." The young man processed Shane's purchase.

"What about all of your food items? Why are the shelves so empty?"

"I guess you haven't been by the grocery store recently." The man handed Shane his receipt.

"No, why?"

"They're out of everything."

"Delivery trucks not running or something?" Shane asked.

"Who knows?" the attendant replied. "Maybe people are buying everything up for the same reason they're hogging up all the gas. Probably think prices will be higher tomorrow."

"Oh." Shane considered the perfect storm which seemed to be brewing. "Maybe I'll get a few snacks while I'm here." He picked up a small basket and looked at the remaining food items on the shelves. He passed on the potted meat but took some jerky. All the top tier candy bars were gone but he was able to get several packages of peanuts, coconut topped donuts, and some off-brand cookies which had been passed over by previous shoppers.

He topped off the cart with some individually packed muffins, granola bars, honey buns, and pizza-flavored Combos. The attendant looked at him as if to ask if he were high. He rang up the horrifying culinary atrocities seldom purchased in such quantities by anyone not under the influence. Shane paid for his selection and left. He tossed the snacks in the back of the Jeep and poured the water in the shrubs on the side of the building. No sooner had he pulled out of the lot than he remembered what he'd forgotten.

"Ah! Her stupid beer!" Already on the other side of the road, he whipped into the Exxon station instead. He stepped out of the car and pulled the door but quickly discovered the shop was closed. Curious, he peered through the door. The lights were out and few items remained on the shelves. Shane felt agitated at having to make a third stop for Lilith's beer. He felt cheated at having to be the responsible one as well as the one putting forth all the effort for her to maintain some semblance of a comfortable lifestyle.

Shane checked his attitude while driving to the Shell station to get beer. "Nobody is perfect. Lilith is as close to the whole package as I'll ever find." He exited the vehicle and let his thoughts wander back to Julianna, his hometown sweetheart that he'd walked away from to be a country music star. Shane felt that old sick feeling of regret; almost nauseating, somewhat frightening, and altogether hopeless.

He looked at the scant availability in the beer cooler. He whispered to himself under his breath.

"Lilith is smart, sexy, and well suited for the celebrity lifestyle. Julianna would have never been happy if I had dragged her to Nashville."

Most of the domestic beers were sold out, but a few six-packs of the more *expensive* beers still remained. He found a carton of Sam Adams and carried it to the register.

"How we doing this evening?" asked the attendant, a thin man with sunken cheeks. The man who'd recognized Shane earlier was gone.

Shane considered pouring out his heart to the frail cashier. "Great," said Shane, instead of elaborating on how the ship of true love had sailed leaving him alone on the shore, cursed to an existence of second best and what could have been.

He took his purchase and returned to the hotel.

Once inside, he was greeted with admonishment.

"What took you so long?" Lilith took the beer.

Shane didn't want a fight, so he ignored the ingratitude and turned up the television.

The screen cut from the male reporter who'd been providing commentary to the Oval Office where President Donovan sat flanked by the American flag and the flag of the President.

"Ladies and gentlemen, I come to you this joyous evening as a general returning from a victorious battle. I'm pleased to announce the plan which my staff, the Congress, and I have been working on for the past several days. We've had a lot of pizza and Chinese food delivered while working tirelessly from early in the morning until late at night. We've gone without sleep, but this crisis demanded nothing less.

"I want you to know that we've heard your grievances. This government is here to serve the entirety of the American people. We do not represent only the old nor only the youth. We do not favor the rich over the poor, but we strive to find fairness for each and every one of you.

"When we announced the previous bailout, our backs were against the wall. Multiple states and cities were in jeopardy of running out of funding to keep basic services like teachers, law enforcement, and fire departments operational. State, local, and federal agencies had made promises that they were becoming unable to fulfill. We had no choice but to intervene.

"It is very difficult to predict how markets will react to large-scale programs like the bailout and we were not able to prepare for the aftershock of such a large infusion of capital into the system.

"However, while we are working on mechanisms to stabilize prices and markets, we are going to provide an individual aid package to each American citizen as well as commodity-based sustenance coupons for Green Card holders and non-residents.

"First, to our citizens, we'll be issuing via the US Treasury, a $5,000.00 aid payment to help you purchase basic goods and services. This payment will help you to offset the rapidly rising costs of food, fuel, and transportation. The initial $5,000.00 is intended to see you through the first quarter of the year. Checks will show up in your mailbox in the same way that you'd receive your tax refund each year. We'll reassess inflationary conditions and determine if further assistance is warranted in April.

"Green Card holders and non-residents will receive EBT cards, which will provide a weekly allotment for basic dietary needs. The amount will vary as we will calculate the total sum needed at the beginning of the week based on the prices of a predetermined basket of staple food items.

"No doubt the pundits will be fast to criticize our plan as being only a band-aid or a quick fix to get us out of the current dilemma. In part, they are correct as this is only the first step in a much larger strategy to combat the crisis.

"The Citizen Aid Package, or CAP, is designed to buy us time, to keep people out of harm's way while we hash out a more permanent resolution.

"In the meantime, your government has a favor to ask of you. Go back to your lives. Return to your jobs. Let's get this train back on the tracks and resume the great ideology referred to by people around the globe as the American Dream. Let's show the rest of the world what resilience is all about. Let's show them what it means to be . . . an American."

"Wow! Five grand to every man, woman, and child? That ought to do it." Lilith twisted the cap off of her second beer bottle.

"Yeah, it'll do it all right. Inflation is going to skyrocket. We ain't seen nothing yet." Shane watched another hour of the news while the television showed the reaction in several of the cities which had experienced the most violent riots. Cameras in Chicago showed people parading through the streets. Protestors in Oakland had stripped away their face masks and were drinking, smoking pot, and dancing in celebrations. In New York, demonstrators hoisted American flags and cheered in triumph for the free money which would soon be theirs.

CHAPTER 13

Let us eat and drink; for to morrow we die.

1 Corinthians 15:32b

January 7th, four days after the announcement of the Citizens Aid Package.

Shane sat at the bar stool nursing a beer while he watched Lilith, Bridgette, and all their friends having a good time Saturday night.

Derrick pulled up the stool next to him. "Must have cost a pretty penny to rent out the Bluebird on a Saturday night."

Shane shook his head. "I didn't even ask. I don't want to know, but it might be the last party we ever have."

"You're still convinced things are going down in flames, huh?"

"Gasoline is $25 a gallon and you have to wait in line all morning to get it. The grocery stores are half stocked. Do you think the bailout is working?"

"Things have to get worse before they can get better. The president said it was only to buy some time so they could come up with a more permanent solution."

Bridgette and Lilith walked up to the bar. "Let's do some shots!" Lilith tugged Shane's arm.

Shane smiled. "I'm going to pass. You go ahead."

Bridgette ran her hand up Derrick's back. "What are you boys talking about?"

Derrick took the tequila shot when Lilith handed it to him. "This thing with the economy."

Bridgette forced one of the small glasses on Shane. "Come on, drink up, Mr. Worrywart. This is your engagement party after all. You need to loosen up anyway."

Shane downed his shot with all the others, winced as a shiver went up his spine, then slid the empty glass across the bar.

"See, that wasn't so bad." Bridgette smiled. "But seriously, I'm asking you to try to relax as your friend but also as Backwoods' manager. Miguel is thinking of going back to his dad's place in Podunk, Texas. A little bird told me that you're the one who has him all worked up about this thing."

Shane stood up from the bar stool. "Miguel doesn't need anyone to get him worked up about anything. The signs are obvious. We got our CAP checks yesterday from the Treasury. I took mine to the bank to try to cash it. Guess what, they had no cash. The teller said I'd have to try back on Monday."

"So, just deposit it and spend it with your credit card or bank card. Since when did $5,000 amount to a drop in the bucket to you anyway?"

He shook his head. "It's not about me. It's about everyone else in the country. This Citizen's Assistance Package is like trying to hold a plane together with chewing gum and paperclips."

Bridgette turned to Lilith. "Where does he come up with this stuff?"

"His father." She rolled her eyes. "He's got a pocket full of one-liners like that, especially if he can apply them to the crisis."

"Well, regardless of what anybody thinks, we all need to work toward getting Miguel calmed down. If he bails on the tour and we have to hire a stand-in, it's going to hurt ticket sales at a time when we'll already be cutting it close." Bridgette sipped from her standard drink, Booker's on the rocks. "Since you had to make such a public showing of the fact that you're off the market, Casey and Miguel are the heartthrobs. Losing Miguel would be a tough blow to all the ladies who pay big bucks to see you guys on stage. We're going to have to charge $200 for the nose bleed section as it is. Huge spikes in fuel prices, food, lodging; I've got a lot of rising overhead to cover and at this point, it's a moving target."

"Maybe we should postpone the tour. Wait until things calm down." Shane sipped his beer.

Bridgette put her hand on her hip. "Oh, no! We're not pulling the plug two weeks before the first show. I worked sixty hours a week all the way up until Christmas Eve to put all the pieces together."

"And we all appreciate your efforts, Bridgette. But you saw what we went through in New York. All I'm saying is that the road would be a bad place to be if things came unglued." Shane really wished Lilith hadn't thrown this party.

Bridgette crossed her arms. "I understand that you meant well, but we could have stayed in our comfy hotel rooms until everything blew over. The situation was finally resolved and that post-apocalyptic scene of us assaulting a taxi driver to get to the airport turned out to be completely unnecessary."

"We didn't know that we were going to be able to get out at the time." Shane finished his beer.

"We had no other reason to believe that it was the end of the world other than you telling us. But, we followed your lead." Her smile was full of venom. "I think it would be better for everybody, yourself included, if you just sit back and enjoy the ride this time. Let me do the driving. It's my job after all."

Shane looked at his phone. "Casey just picked Bobby up from the airport. I'm going to run over there and make sure he's okay."

"Have them come here," Lilith suggested.

"Bobby just got out of jail. He'll need to decompress for a day or two before he's ready to go out." Shane put his jacket on.

"You're leaving me? At our engagement party?"

"I'll be right back. I'm just going to let Bobby know that we're here for him. Welcome him home, that sort of thing."

"You're going to drive?"

"I'll take a taxi over there. Casey will bring me back."

"Don't be long." She kissed him on the lips.

"Take care of that thing with Miguel for me." The corners of Brigitte's mouth turned up, but her eyes burned with all the viciousness of a mob boss.

Shane ignored her request, waved to Derrick, and walked out the door.

***

Twenty minutes later, the cab dropped Shane off at Bobby's apartment. He knocked.

"Come in," Bobby called from inside.

Shane stepped through the door and hugged the giant of a man. "So good to have you home."

Casey was there and Miguel had just arrived.

Bobby replied, "It's good to be home."

"I appreciate everything you did for us." Shane took a seat on the couch.

"I'd do it all over again. Stan would say the same thing. Casey told me about the memorial service. I wish I could have been there."

"Lilith is having a party over at the Bluebird, celebrating our engagement. You boys are all welcome to come," Shane offered.

"Is Bridgette there?" Miguel asked.

"Of course," Shane sighed.

"Then I'll pass," he replied. "I told her I'm heading out on Monday. She got me confused with Derrick, thought she could bully me into sticking around. I told her to forget about it. She thinks she can still pull off a tour."

"What do you think, Shane?" Casey inquired.

"No way. Even if we could, we'd lose money. People might have an extra five grand in their pocket right now, but they'll use that to stock up on basic supplies if they know what's good for them."

"If we all stick together on this, do you think she'll back down, cancel the tour?" asked Miguel.

Shane shook his head. "In all honesty, if society hasn't completely imploded by the time we're supposed to leave, I think she'll try to rebrand the concerts as Derrick Collum from Backwoods."

"You think people would go to that?" Miguel furrowed his brow.

"Some would. I think Bridgette would strip it down, change to smaller venues, but I guess she could milk it for something."

"But you're not getting on the bus, right?" Casey looked at Shane.

"No. No way. Not after New York."

"Are you going to tell Bridgette?" Miguel asked.

"Nope. I've told her I think we should cancel the tour, but she doesn't want to listen. I'm not going to say anything else about it. I don't want to give her time to reframe the tour as the Derrick Collum show. What are you going to do, Casey?"

"Miguel invited me to go to Texas. Sounds safer than sticking around here. What about you?"

"Hunker down in Belle Meade I guess. It's a

gated community. I've been stocking up on canned goods. I've gone to the grocery every day since we got back. I spent all day Thursday calling around for ammo."

"Find anything?" Bobby asked.

"Found two cases of target load for my shotgun but had to drive all the way to Murfreesboro to get it. Couldn't find anything for my 9mm or my AR.

"Bobby, you're welcome to come stay with us if things get bad."

"Thanks. I might take you up on that." The big man smiled.

"You should come to Texas with Casey and me," Miguel offered. "You, too, Shane. We'll make room. I wouldn't put much stock in that gate at the entrance of your community. Bobby could lean on it and rip that flimsy thing off the hinges."

Shane laughed. "Thanks, but I wouldn't do that to your folks. My other half can be a tough customer at times."

Miguel sat back in the chair. "She's not half as bad as Bridgette. I'd invite Derrick, but she ain't coming."

Casey stood up. "I need to get going. I have to figure out what I'm going to take, and what I'm going to leave behind. If it's as bad as you guys say, I may never see my place again."

"Me, too. Casey, think you could drop me at the Bluebird?" Shane also got up.

"Sure. Come on."

Shane shook hands with Bobby. "Good to have you back."

CHAPTER 14

Then I heard a voice in the midst of the four living creatures saying, "A quart of wheat for a day's wages, and three quarts of barley for a day's wages, and do not harm the oil and the wine."

Revelation 6:6 MEV

January 11th, four days after Shane and Lilith's engagement party at the Bluebird Café.

Shane waved at the delivery driver and brought the cardboard box to the kitchen early Wednesday morning.
"What's that?" Lilith sipped her coffee.
He pulled the packaging paper away and held the item up for her to see. "A water filter."
"You going camping?"

"No. I thought if things get bad we could use it to filter water from the pool."

"For what?"

"Drinking."

"Shane, our whole guest room is filling up with this junk. The canned goods, the camping food, two cases of bullets . . ."

"Shotgun shells," he corrected.

"Whatever. The point is, you said we had to cut back. I've been trying to do my part, but you keep buying more stuff."

"Everything I've bought costs less than half of what you spent on renting out the Bluebird, not to mention the catering bill and the liquor bill."

"That was for us. And don't forget all the money you spent on those stupid coins."

"Spent? How about invested? Gold has doubled since I bought those."

"You didn't know it was going up when you bought it." She refilled her coffee cup and picked up her phone. "It could just as easily go back down tomorrow." Lilith left the room. It was her usual way of making sure she got the last word in an argument.

Shane took three deep breaths to calm himself and opened the package. He chose to focus on his new gadget and let the argument go.

Lilith returned sooner than she usually would after a spat. "Bridgette needs to borrow some money. Can we lend her $500?"

"Borrow money? Derrick makes almost twice as much as me. Why does she need money?"

"It's not like that. Her bank is closed and the

grocery store is not taking credit cards. She can write us a check."

"Her bank is closed on a Wednesday? Is today a holiday?"

"Evidently. She said it's some banking holiday."

"A banking holiday? It's January 11th. There's no holiday today. Why wouldn't the grocery store take her credit card?" Shane processed the limited information.

"I don't know. Can you just open the safe and get some cash out for her?"

Shane slowly put the pieces together while he fulfilled Lilith's request. He opened the safe, pulled out the small wooden box containing his cash and counted out $500 to Lilith.

"Thanks, I'll be back." She grabbed her purse and keys, then headed for the door.

Shane hurried to the great room and turned on the television, navigating straight to the financial news station.

A reporter stood on the floor of the eerily quiet NYSE. "If you're just now joining us, the SEC pulled the plug on trading for the day before markets had a chance to get rolling. The S&P had already triggered two circuit breakers by 9:50 this morning after dropping 7% within seconds of the opening bell, then another 6% after reopening from the level one halt. The SEC decided not to let trading resume after the second breaker was taken out so quickly.

The reasoning behind the precipitous crash was a perfect storm of volatility and inability of the government to convince investors that they are able to evade a systemic economic collapse. While the causes are numerous, the initial catalyst for this morning's carnage was the bond market.

"The Treasury held their first note auction of the year today and no one showed up. I think we all knew that confidence in the dollar was waning, but today's revelation proves that America's currency is dead. Not only did foreign sovereign entities fail to purchase the instruments once considered the benchmark for reliability, but neither did domestic institutional investors.

"The rumor mill has suggested that maturing bills, notes, and bonds were being purchased in greater and greater quantities by a black-box fund run by the President's Working Group on Financial Markets, AKA the Plunge Protection Team. Supposedly, the market had already displayed a lack of interest in US debt, but this government buying spree had served to keep the loss of popularity swept under the rug.

"But this morning, the proverbial tide has gone out and we find that Treasury-issued debt was indeed swimming with no bathing suit. This epiphany triggered a string of dominos which have yet to cease toppling.

"First, Russia and Canada have joined OPEC in declaring that they can no longer accept US dollars as payment for oil. This limits the US to consuming only oil from domestic production or to purchase the precious commodity in one of the recognized currencies which are also not for sale in exchange for US dollars. Most global forex markets have completely delisted the US dollar from their exchange boards.

"Also not accepting dollars are world gold retailers. The yellow metal's last stated price was $11,000, but none of the major gold markets are recognizing that price. Even so, the favored commodity is gaining fast against the Euro, Pound, and RMB.

"The Federal Reserve, in anticipation of a further run on accounts and paper currency, formally declared a banking holiday in the US, mandating that all banks operating on US soil close for business by 10:30 AM. Most banks were all too eager to comply and many had their doors locked before 10:00 this morning.

"Credit card companies and banks who issue plastic have frozen accounts. Financial institutions are citing that account holders will have no means to repay balances until the crisis is resolved and a replacement currency issued to fill in for the failed US dollar.

"The White House has not issued a statement about today's pandemonium, but sources inside say an announcement is forthcoming."

Shane stood in front of the television with his mouth hanging open. He muttered to himself, "A lamentation of black swans."

He quickly took out his phone and called Lilith. A computerized voice said, "All circuits are busy. Your call cannot be completed at this time."

"You've got to be kidding me." Shane tried frantically to call her several more times. Finally, he resorted to sending a text. *Come straight home after you leave Bridgette's.*

He looked at the time on his phone. "Thirty more minutes before the local midday news." Nevertheless, Shane clicked through the local channels.

One of them was airing the midday news early to cover Nashville's reaction to the markets in turmoil. The camera showed people in long lines trying to get cash out of ATMs. Shane muted the sound, ignoring the commentary while he watched the scenes from around his city. He continued to try reaching Lilith.

Finally, his phone rang. "Hey, Dad. Can I call you back? I'm trying to get a hold of Lilith."

"No need. I'll make this quick. It's time to come home, Son. Pack your stuff, put your girlfriend in the truck, and come home. You don't need anything except your guns and your gold; maybe a change of socks. Don't dilly dally, Shane. This is it. This is the big one we've been waiting for."

"I'll talk to Lilith about it."

"Don't talk. Just do. I know you're a grown man, but I'm not asking this time. Come home."

"I stocked up the house. We've got canned goods, ammo, water filters, I think we'll be okay here for a while."

"Nashville is going to devolve into a war zone in the next forty-eight to seventy-two hours. You need to get out while you can. No amount of preparation is going to make staying a viable option."

"We're outside of the city, around six miles from the 440. I doubt we'll have much trouble where I'm at."

"You live where all the other big money lives. When desperate people run out of food and water, where do you think they're going to look for resources? Do you think they'll go scratch around in the hood, or do you think they'll come to see if the rich folks have anything worth taking?"

"My neighborhood is gated. Belle Mead has its own police department. If all else fails, I've got a shotgun, an AR-15, and a pistol."

"If you stay, you're gonna need them. When the paper-thin façade of civility melts away, those cops are gonna have to take care of their own families. You'll be on your own.

"This isn't something you want to try to ride out in a city like Nashville. The greater metropolitan area has close to two million people. Our little town doesn't even have three thousand. Please, Son. I'm begging you."

"Thanks, Dad. I'll mull it over. I'll call you back tonight."

"Okay, I love you." Paul Black ended the call.

Shane desperately continued to try contacting Lilith. Finally, the call went through.

Lilith answered, "Hey, baby. Everybody is going crazy. I don't know what's wrong with people."

"Where are you?"

"Kroger."

"You need to leave now."

"We're leaving. Bridgette was waiting for me at the grocery store when, all of a sudden, some woman started taking stuff out of her cart. She'd gotten the last of a few items, so it wasn't like she could just go back and get more. Anyway, Bridgette tried to protect her stuff and the woman attacked her. She's all scratched up. We're in line to check out, then we're going to file a police report."

"Don't bother with that. You need to come home now."

"I will, but I'm going to stay with Bridgette. I'll tell her you said to forget about the police report."

"What Kroger are you at? The one on Harding Pike?" Shane opened the safe and took out his Glock model 19.

"Yes."

"Call me when you're in the car and leaving the parking lot. If the call won't go through, try sending me a text." His flimsy clip-on, in-the-waist-band holster was all he had for concealed carry. He'd meant to upgrade to something sturdier but had never gotten around to it. It would have to do for now.

"Why wouldn't the call go through?"

"People are panicking, trying to call each other, and jamming up the network. I tried to call you like twenty times before I got through."

"Okay, if I can't call, I'll text."

Shane hung up, shoved his phone in his pocket, and then clipped the holster and pistol inside his jeans. He quickly slipped into his jacket, stepped into his boots, and snatched his truck keys. Once in the cab of his Sierra, he called Derrick but got the computer. "All circuits are busy. Your call cannot be completed at this time."

Shane started the engine and raced toward the Kroger. He did a double take when he passed the first gas station. "$65 a gallon? You've got to be kidding me!"

Even so, people were lined up into the road trying to purchase the precious commodity. The next filling station he passed was not nearly so orderly. Evidently, two motorists had attempted to enter the same line at the same time. Each of them were out of their vehicles and squabbling in the road while drivers behind them beeped horns and yelled out the window.

Another car honked. This time it was next to Shane's truck. He swerved, barely avoiding a collision. While gawking at the melee, he'd inadvertently drifted into the other lane. He refocused and sharpened his gaze, paying attention to only the traffic around him.

Kroger's lot looked like a scene from Black Friday. It was filled to capacity with angry drivers yelling at each other over parking spaces.

Shane parked at the far corner of the adjacent shopping center. He looked at the Office Depot which, in stark contrast to the Kroger, had no activity. "I guess no one is interested in office supplies at a time like this." He pulled his jacket over the handle of his gun and exited the vehicle. Shane checked his phone once more to see if Lilith had messaged him but saw nothing.

Shane sprinted toward the grocery store. Once inside, he quickly picked Bridgette and Lilith out of the crowd. They'd completed their checkout, but the manager was detaining them.

"I understand, ma'am, but we need you to stay until the police arrived." He stood in front of

Bridgette's cart.

"What's the problem?" Shane asked.

"I didn't know you were coming here," Lilith said. "Why didn't you tell me?"

"I didn't want you to hang around waiting for me, in case you left before I arrived."

The store manager seemed agitated at having to wait for them to finish their conversation before he could answer Shane. "This lady is our only witness to the incident. We need her to stay to talk to the police."

"Don't you have cameras?"

"Yes, but we need her statement."

Shane nudged the man out of the way with his body. "I'm sorry, she has to leave now."

The manager became more forceful. "She cannot leave." He resumed his place in front of the cart.

"She was the one who was attacked. It's her discretion if she wants to press charges or not."

"Not exactly," said the manager.

"What do you mean?" Shane lowered his eyebrows.

"It's unclear who the aggressor was in the altercation."

"What?" Bridgette screeched. "What are you talking about? Are you accusing me of starting the fight?"

Shane saw that the situation would only get worse if they hung around. He pushed the manager out of the way and led Bridgette's cart. He pointed at the manager. "If we're still here when the police arrive, I'll have you charged with false imprisonment, for detaining these girls. And trust me, we can afford much better lawyers than you can."

The man scowled at Shane.

"Let's go." Shane pulled the cart from the front, with Bridgette and Lilith trailing behind. "Where's your car?"

Bridgette indicated toward the back of the lot. "Over there. Thank you for getting us out of there. He was trying to have me locked up! The nerve some people have!"

"Let's move faster." Shane tried to hurry the girls along.

Once they reached Bridgette's Mercedes SUV, he opened the hatch and rushed to put her groceries in. "Go straight home, Bridgette."

"But I need to get gas."

"Not today. It's chaos."

"The only cash I have is what Lilith gave me. Gas could be $100 a gallon tomorrow."

"Go home and stay there. You don't need gas if you don't go anywhere." He slammed the hatch shut and took Lilith by the hand.

"My BMW is that way." Lilith pulled away.

"You're riding with me. We'll come to get it later." Shane took her hand once more.

"I'm not leaving without my car." She glared at him.

"Fine. I'll walk you to your car, then you can drive me to the truck. I'll follow you home."

**

Once home, Shane intentionally pulled in behind

Lilith rather than beside her vehicle. The Sierra would have to be moved in order for her to get out.

She seemed not to notice. At least she didn't give him any grief about it. "I'm going to take a bubble bath, try to relax. That was just insane!" She walked into the house.

"Sure. Take your time." Shane paused outside. He closed the door and meandered about in the front yard, looking at his home from a different perspective. The neo-classical brick home was sturdy. Stairs led up either side of the porch to the main level which was elevated five feet from the ground. Even the Roman pillars on the porch gave the home the feeling of being a fortress. The four floor-to-ceiling windows were the obvious weak points from the front of the house. But even they were narrow, limiting the vulnerability.

Shane's phone rang. "Derrick, is everything okay?"

"Yeah, bud. Thanks to you. I appreciate what you did for Bridgette. I didn't even know what was going on until she called."

"No problem. You'd have done the same for me. I know she doesn't like to take orders, but you need to make her stay home. I understand what it's like to try managing someone who's high-maintenance, but things are bad out there."

Derrick exhaled. "Lilith is high-maintenance. Bridgette is about five levels up from that. I'm not even sure what they call it."

Shane laughed. "We all like having a pit bull on our side when she's negotiating a contract with the record company."

Derrick sighed. "I could handle a pit bull, but Bridgette's more like a velociraptor. And it's not like she has a switch so she only gets prehistoric when she's working. Trust me, you don't know how good you've got it."

"Do what you've got to do. Just don't let her go back out."

"I won't. I'll have a talk with her when she gets home."

"She's not home yet?" Shane asked.

"No. But I just got off the phone with her. She's on her way."

"We're two miles further from Kroger than you. Plus we had to cross the parking lot. She should have beat us home."

"Yeah, I think she's going to try to find some gas."

Shane shook his head. "That's a mistake. She should have gone straight home."

"I know, but what can you do?"

"Stay safe. I'll talk to you later." Shane ended the call and resumed assessing his home for security concerns.

CHAPTER 15

History is a record of "effects" the vast majority of which nobody intended to produce.

Joseph Schumpeter

Still standing in the front yard Wednesday afternoon, Shane listened to the sound of sirens whining in the distance. The country club served as a buffer between his home and the main road, Harding Pike. However, the noise of emergency vehicles easily carried over.

Shane dialed Bobby's number, unsure how many attempts it would take him to get through. "All circuits are busy. Your call cannot be completed at this time."

Shane huffed and tried texting his friend. *Things*

are getting worse. Just got back from the grocery. People are coming unglued. Come on over if you want.

Bobby's reply came quickly. *I think I'll take you up on that offer. I'm a little closer to downtown than I'd like to be. Should I bring anything?*

Shane typed away on his phone. *Guns and food.*

Shane's phone rang. "Derrick, what's up?"

"I've been trying to get through. It's Bridgette. She had an accident trying to get gas."

"An accident?"

"Yeah, claims some guy in a truck tried to cut her off. She's bawling like a baby and wants me to come help her out."

"She needs to get in the car and leave."

"Evidently, the guy won't let her leave. He says it's her fault."

"I guess she'll have to wait for the cops then."

"It's a little more complicated than that," Derrick replied.

"How so?"

"Bridgette was so stressed out by the thing at Kroger that she got into one of her bottles of wine."

"So what? A couple of sips isn't going to make her blow over the limit."

"She chugged the whole bottle."

Shane ran his hand over his face. "How did she even open a bottle of wine in the car?"

"She carries an opener in her purse. It's a special one that she likes. She won't use anything else so she always has it with her."

Shane knew Derrick was fishing but he wasn't going to take the bait. "Sorry about that, brother."

"Would you mind riding down there with me? Maybe if the guy sees us, he'll turn out to be a Backwoods fan. Maybe I can just offer to pay for the damages, and he'll let us leave before the cops show up."

"You're the front man. If he won't let it go at your request, I don't know how I can help."

"For moral support. You can stay in the truck if you want."

Shane set his teeth together. "Down where?"

"Past the state park on Highway 100."

"What is she doing so far south?"

"The station by our house is already out of gas. They locked up and went home. She thought it would be less hectic if she went south because it's further from downtown. This would mean a lot to me."

Shane pressed his lips together. "I guess I can come along."

"I'm two minutes out. I'll pick you up."

"I'll be out front." Shane went inside to tell Lilith where he was going. He slid the keys to his truck on the kitchen counter. Lilith could move the truck if she had to get out in an emergency, but he didn't want it to be overly easy for her to leave. He opened the bathroom door. "Bridgette is in another mess. I'm riding with Derrick to help her out. You just stay put."

Lilith lifted her head off the back of the tub, causing the towel she was using for a pillow to fall into the water. "What happened?"

"I'll text you the details. Derrick is picking me up right now. I've got to go." He closed the door before she could object.

Derrick blew the horn of his black Escalade. Shane hustled down the stairs, opened the door, and got in the passenger's seat.

"Thanks for coming with me." Derrick raced out of the neighborhood and to the main road.

Shane glanced at Derrick's fuel gauge. "An eighth of a tank. You're not in very good shape yourself."

"You're right. We should have been more proactive. But it's less than 10 miles from here. I've got plenty to get there and back."

Shane didn't say anything else on the drive. Derrick got them to Bridgette's location in record time.

Derrick rolled out of the SUV and embraced Bridgette who was still arguing with the other driver, making matters worse. Shane got out and said to Derrick, "Take her over behind the SUV. I'll try talking to the guy."

Shane stepped up to the man. "Sir, I'm so sorry about this. What can we do to make it right?"

The man had a thick gray beard which matched his gray work clothes. His name tag indicated that his name was Steve. "Nothin'. Police will sort it out when they get here. Just keep that girl calm. She's a mess."

Shane looked at the damage to the man's pickup. "Are you a mechanic?"

"What if I am?"

"I was just thinking, if we worked this out between us, maybe you could get the work done cheaper and keep the rest for yourself."

"I don't want any bribes."

"It's not a bribe. It's just skipping the long insurance process. The way things are going, you might not ever see a dime from the insurance company."

"Why's that?"

"Banks are closed. Credit card companies are shut down." Shane pointed at the dent on the quarter panel. "A shop will probably charge five-hundred to fix that. I'll give you a thousand."

"Make it two."

Shane knew the man had him over a barrel, but he didn't want to give up that much. "I don't have two thousand."

"How much you got?"

"Probably fourteen or fifteen hundred."

"Give me fifteen."

"And you'll leave right now? Before the cops come?"

"Yep. Let's see it."

Shane quickly counted out the money.

"Thought you said you didn't have two thousand." The man took the stack of bills and watched Shane tuck the rest back into his pocket.

"I don't have two thousand to give you. I need the rest of this for groceries."

"Well, I only agreed to fifteen because I was being nice."

"Sounds like you're trying to hustle us," Derrick walked up.

The man pulled a small semi-automatic out of his pocket. "So now you two planning' on double teamin' me? I don't think so. How about you pull the rest of that money out of your pocket?" The man pointed the pistol at Derrick. "You, too, pretty boy. Go on and empty your pockets while you're at it."

Shane used the split second that the man had his attention on Derrick to pull his own pistol. His stomach clenched up, his hands became like ice, and time froze. Shane pulled the trigger, hitting the man in the abdomen.

With pained eyes, the man pointed the small pistol in Shane's direction and fired two rounds. Shane winced in terror, but the man had missed. Shane wasted no time in lining up his sights with the man's head. He fired two more rounds and the man dropped to the ground.

Bridgette screamed.

Shane pointed at Derrick. "Put her in the Mercedes and get her out of here. I'll follow you in the Escalade." Shane quickly retrieved his money from the man's back pocket. He rushed toward Derrick's truck. He felt dizzy and nauseous all of a sudden. An overdose of adrenaline was making him sick. Shane bent over and vomited.

"Are you okay?" Derrick asked.

"I'm fine. Just get out of here. And stay off Highway 100. We need to take the back roads home." Shane continued to dry-heave as he started the vehicle and drove off.

Derrick led the way, taking Sneed Road to Hillsboro, which brought them in the back way to the neighborhood.

Once they arrived, Shane parked the Escalade next to his Sierra and got out.

Derrick rolled down his window. "I'm going to

get her home. I'll come to get the Escalade later."

Shane leaned on the top of the car. "You shouldn't go home. If someone got her plate number, that's the first place they'll look."

"I didn't do anything wrong." Bridgette protested. "I just want to go home."

Shane looked past Derrick. "You were drunk driving, and you hit somebody at a gas station. What do you mean you didn't do anything wrong?"

"I mean, I didn't murder anybody."

"Murder?" Shane's pulse quickened. "That guy was going to kill your husband. I saved his life."

"You didn't handle the situation right." Bridgette sat back in her seat.

Lilith came storming out into the driveway wearing her robe. "Bridgette! Are you okay? What happened?"

"Your trigger-happy husband tried to get us all killed. That's what happened."

Shane's blood began to boil. He looked at Derrick. "On second thought, you better go ahead and take her home. And call Barry. Don't let her talk to the police until he gets there."

Bridgette yelled, "If they ask, I'll tell them who killed that man. Don't expect us to take the fall for that."

Shane pointed. "Derrick, get her out of here."

Derrick looked remorseful. "If the cops show up asking questions, I'll at least give you a heads up."

"What is she talking about? Why did she say you killed someone?" Lilith asked.

"I'll explain. But for now, we have to pack a bag. It's time to go."

"Go where?"

"To Sylva. I can't get caught up in an investigation while the country is melting down. Jail is not the place to ride this thing out. When the cops show up at Derrick's, Bridgette is going to blab about everything that happened."

"Shane, we're not going to your parents'."

"I am. You can stay here until the monsters show up if you want, but I'm leaving in twenty minutes. I'm not waiting around."

"So you're going to abandon me?" Lilith trailed behind him.

Shane opened the safe. He began putting his rifle and shotgun into a soft carrying case. "I'm not abandoning you. I've invited you to come along. If you refuse, I'm not going to add kidnapping to my list of charges."

A knock came to the door. Shane's heart skipped a beat. Panic took over. His mouth went dry.

"Who is that?" Lilith grabbed his arm.

Shane drew his pistol and rushed to the front window. He peered out and let out a sigh of relief. "It's Bobby."

"What is he doing here?"

"I asked him to stay with us until things calmed down." Shane made his way to the door.

"Why?"

"Because he lives near all the danger and because we can use an extra set of eyes and ears, not to mention a little muscle." Shane opened the door. "Change of plans, big guy."

"Oh?"

Shane let him in. He led the way back to the

bedroom and continued packing while he explained the events which had transpired since they last spoke. "You should come with me."

Bobby looked at Lilith. "You're not coming?"

Lilith looked worried. She twisted the belt of her robe nervously but said nothing.

Shane hoped she'd come, but couldn't waste time. "If you're going to change your mind, you better start packing. I'm leaving in fifteen minutes."

"I can't even get dressed that fast," she argued.

"Should have thought about that five minutes ago." Shane lugged some bags out to the truck. Bobby helped him load up.

Fifteen minutes later, Shane clapped his hands. "Come on! Let's go!"

"Wait!" Lilith yelled.

"No more waiting. We should have already been gone. Put your shoes on. We're leaving now." Shane closed her suitcase and zipped it up.

She stepped into untied running shoes. Lilith hadn't even put on socks. Her hair was still damp from her bath and she had on no makeup. "Leaving the house looking like this is really the low point of the crisis for me."

Shane handed her suitcase to Bobby and grabbed the rest of Lilith's luggage. "Then you're doing better than Bobby and me."

"You'll drive your truck, Bobby?" Shane took the suitcase from the giant and put it in the back of his Sierra.

"Yeah, I've got a full tank." Bobby got into his F-150 and closed the door.

Shane backed out of the drive and drove east.

He'd follow Harding Place until it became Donaldson Pike. From there, he could pick up I-40, which would take him home to the mountains.

CHAPTER 16

The masses do not like those who surpass them in any regard. The average man envies and hates those who are different.

Ludwig von Mises

Three hours later, Shane began to breathe a little easier. He'd received no notice from Derrick and the trip had been uneventful. He checked the rearview to see that Bobby was still close behind him. The sun hung low behind them. Up ahead were the Appalachian Mountains. They seemed to Shane a place of refuge from the chaos he'd left hours before. Other drivers whizzed past, driving erratically, but Shane kept to the right lane and let them pass.

Lilith sat slumped back in her seat with a sour

expression. She checked her phone.

"Any news from Bridgette?"

She looked once more. "No. She says no one has come by. We could have just stayed home."

"That wasn't an option. We should have left weeks ago when my dad first invited us. That scene at the gas station could have been avoided altogether."

"So how is this going to work? You and me, I mean?"

"We'll have the preacher marry us, and we can live in the little house, where my dad's office is."

"Like some hillbilly shotgun wedding?"

"It's not a shotgun wedding if all parties are willing participants." Shane laughed. Even with no makeup and her hair a mess, Lilith was so beautiful that even her poutiness came off as cute.

She crossed her arms and slumped lower into the seat. She'd kicked off her shoes and had her feet resting on the dash. "Do they even sell wedding gowns in Sylva?"

"People get married there all the time. I'm sure wedding dresses are available."

"It won't be like a boutique in Nashville. And who will cater it?" She rolled her eyes. "I'm going to look like Elly May Clampett. And our reception is going to look like the trough where she fed all her critters."

Shane bit his tongue to keep from laughing.

She gave a sigh of exasperation and looked out the window. "It doesn't matter. None of my friends will be there."

Shane let his mind drift. He dreamed of a simpler

life. Perhaps pulling Lilith out of Nashville would make her more amiable. Maybe it was the fast-paced lifestyle of the music industry which made her so particular. It had certainly affected him for the worse. He welcomed the change.

A few miles later, Lilith sat up and began putting her shoes on.

Shane glanced over. "We've still got about an hour and a half before we get there."

"I need to go to the restroom."

"We're in Knoxville right now. Can you wait until we get through? This isn't a very safe place to stop."

"How do you know?"

"Because it's a big city."

"It's not as big as Nashville."

"And we barely escaped there with our lives."

"I've got to go. We need to stop now. Look, this exit has a Pilot. They're usually cleaner than most other places. And they have a store."

"If we stop, we're not buying anything."

"Can you at least get me some beer? You're dragging me out to the middle of nowhere to live with Puritans for the rest of my life. This might be the last chance I ever have to get a drink." She pulled down the visor mirror and attempted to do something with her hair. "I'll probably have Kool-Aid instead of Cristal at my shotgun wedding. I don't think I'm asking too much. Regardless, I'm going to wet my pants if you don't pull off now."

Shane frowned and put on his blinker. He checked his rearview to see Bobby flash his lights, indicating that he understood they were stopping.

Shane followed the exit but quickly changed lanes. "Sorry, baby. Pilot is a madhouse. It's probably one of the last places that still has gas this late in the day. We'll keep driving and look for something less chaotic."

"Okay, but hurry up."

Half a mile later, Shane pointed to the left. "There's a mini-mart."

"It looks filthy. At least Pilot is going to have a clean bathroom. That's the whole reason we got off at this exit in the first place. Can we please just turn around? We can park across the street if you want. We'll stay out of the commotion."

Reluctantly, Shane made a U-turn and went back to the Pilot Travel Center. He pulled off the road and onto the shoulder across the street from the filling station. He watched as Bobby parked behind him.

Lilith opened the door and rushed across the road to the travel center. Shane looked at Bobby. "Can you keep an eye on the vehicles?"

"Sure." Bobby got out to stretch.

"Thanks." Shane took enough money to buy a few things and stuck his wallet in the glove box. He'd learned his lesson the hard way about advertising how much cash he had. Shane sprinted to keep up with Lilith.

He followed her inside. To his surprise, the line at the cash register wasn't nearly as long as the line at the pumps. He mumbled to himself, "I guess people don't have to come inside until they get to a pump." Shane looked over the grocery shelves, which were all but bare. Non-food items appeared to be fully stocked. A rack of pre-paid cell phones caught Shane's eye. "I could use one of these to stay in touch with Derrick. If I use my phone, I'll be broadcasting my location to the cops." Shane took a phone and squeezed past some other shoppers in the crowded mini-mart to get to the beer cooler. Once again, all the regular beer was sold out but a few cartons of high-end ales and lagers remained.

Shane looked at the price which had been written on a sticky note. "$40 for a six-pack. Wow!" He opened the door and took two. "I guess cash won't be good for anything else anyway."

Shane brought his purchases to the counter. Even the money he had taken from the truck, he held low so not to display it to curious onlookers. After about 10 minutes in line, he paid the attendant and walked toward the door.

Lilith was waiting for him. "You only bought 2 six-packs?"

"Yeah, we can't cart a bunch of booze into my mom and dad's house."

"We'll keep it in the truck."

"It'll freeze and explode. Then, my truck will stink for the rest of my life. This might be the last vehicle I ever own."

"It might be the last grocery store we ever go to also. Give me some money. I'm going to get more beer, and maybe some candy."

Shane shook his head. "We've got nowhere to put the beer."

"I'll hide it in my room. I'll sneak in a few bottles at a time and stash them in the closet." She poked him in the gut with her open hand.

Shane pressed his lips together and handed her the rest of the cash he'd brought.

Lilith pointed to the beer in Shane's hand. "Take that to the truck and come back so you can help me carry the rest."

Shane looked around to make sure he saw no signs of trouble before leaving her alone. He took the beer and hurried back to the vehicle.

"Mind if I hit the head real quick?" asked Bobby.

"Sure. But Lilith is buying more beer. Can you just check up on her when you go in?"

"You got it."

Shane opened his new phone and went through the activation process. He powered on his old phone and quickly put it on airplane mode. He found Derrick's number and sent him a text on the new phone. *Hey, it's me. Has anybody been by to ask questions?*

While he waited for a response, Shane entered his other important numbers into the new phone.

Derrick replied shortly thereafter. *No one has been by. Riots downtown. Setting fires. I think they've got all they can handle. Still too soon to say for sure but maybe we got lucky.*

Feeling relieved, Shane simply texted back, *Thanks!*

Bobby returned. "Everything is cool inside. I'll watch the cars if you want to go back inside with Lilith. She's standing in line."

"Be right back." Shane stepped a little lighter with the prospect of not getting hit with a murder or manslaughter charge.

He smiled widely at Lilith who was paying the

cashier. He took four cartons leaving Lilith only two to carry. "Derrick said no one has been by looking for us."

"Great. We left Nashville for nothing." She rolled her eyes.

"I wouldn't say it's for nothing. He said downtown looks like a war zone."

"We don't live downtown."

Shane knew the tumult would spread but didn't want an argument, so he let it go. They left the store and crossed the lot. Five young men were walking toward the travel center.

One of them looked at Shane. "Wow! You guys having a party or what?"

Shane ignored him and kept walking.

The boys stepped in front of him. "Hey, my friend asked if you're having a party," said another.

"Come on." Shane signaled for Lilith to follow him as he tried to walk around the men.

They quickly cut him off, encircling him and Lilith.

"Bro, we're just trying to be friendly here. You ain't gotta be a jerk," said the husky one.

"Yeah," said the tall skinny one. "How about you let us get one of them beers, and we'll forget about the offense."

Not wanting to get into a shootout over a beer, Shane sat one of the six-packs on the ground. "Sure. Help yourselves. We didn't mean to offend you."

"All right!" The young men clapped and whistled as they stepped closer to claim their prize.

"Enjoy, guys." Shane motioned for Lilith to follow him.

One of the boys opened his beer and took a swig. "Whoa! Whoa!" He stepped in front of Lilith.

Shane sat his beer on the ground and prepared to draw his gun. They could have the beer, but if they put a finger on Lilith, he'd kill them all. "Don't touch her."

"Relax, homie. I just wanted to get a look at that ring. Is that real?" The sun was setting but still offered enough light for the giant gemstone to sparkle like a miniature disco-ball.

"Of course it's real," Lilith snapped.

"You guys must be part of the one percent. Everybody says all this stuff happening is your fault." One of the young men glared at Shane and lifted his hoodie to reveal the handle of a gun.

Shane tried to calculate if he could beat him to the draw. He looked around at the other four men. Two of them had also lifted their jackets to reveal pistols tucked in their pants.

"Wow, a beer will take care of snubbing us in the parking lot, but all this?" The husky one motioned to the long lines at the pumps. "That's gonna cost you. Let me get that ring."

"No way!" Lilith pulled one of the beer bottles out of the carton and slung it at the fat guy.

He drew his pistol. "You're a feisty one, aren't you?" He stepped closer to her.

Shane got ready to draw if Fat Boy touched Lilith. "Give him the ring, Lilith. It's just a rock. I'll get you another one."

"No! I'm not giving up my ring." She drew another bottle and held it over her head.

The fat boy raised his gun, a snub nose revolver.

He pulled the hammer back. "If you hit me with that bottle, I swear I'll shoot you."

She slowly lowered the glass container.

"Good girl, now let me get that rock." He grabbed her hand.

Shane's stomach twisted into a knot once more. His only advantage was that all of their eyes were on Fat Boy, Lilith, and the three-carat diamond sparkling in the fading light of day. Once again, time slowed to a crawl. Shane drew his pistol, leveled it at Fat Boy and fired.

He hit the husky man in the neck, then lowered the muzzle and shot once more. The second round sunk into the big guy's torso and knocked him to the ground. His pistol went off and Shane ducked. He turned to see the other two men with guns aiming at him. He saw the muzzles of their guns flash. Shane returned fire. More gunshots popped off around him. He wasn't sure where they were coming from. He focused on eliminating the two who were shooting at him.

The tall thin hoodlum held a compact semi-auto. He fired twice more at Shane. Shane hit him in the chest and sent him to the ground. Shane turned to address the threat of the other man who'd been shooting at him from close range, but he was already face down in a growing pool of blood.

The peripheral gunfire ceased. Shane looked around. Bobby was charging toward him, his .45 in hand with a thin wisp of smoke trailing out of the barrel. "You're hit, brother." Bobby placed his pistol on the ground and looked at Shane's arm.

Shane looked down to see a hole in the left arm

of his jacket. Blood streamed from the opening, turning the sleeve of his coat red. He quickly looked around for Lilith. She lay on her back near the husky man.

Shane felt a sharp burning pain in his bicep but darted toward Lilith. Her sweatshirt was covered in blood. She'd been hit in the gut.

Shane put his hand gently under her head. "Baby, can you hear me?"

She batted her eyes. Her voice was weak. "Yes. I'm so sorry, Shane. If I hadn't gone back for more…"

"No, don't think that. You're going to be okay." He looked at her stomach. Her hoodie was sopping wet with blood.

"I don't know, baby," came her faint reply. "I love you, Shane. You were always good to me. Better than I deserved. I know I wasn't always the easiest person to deal with."

"Don't say that, Lilith. You're fantastic. And you're going to be a wonderful wife." Shane looked at Bobby. "We need to get her to a hospital."

Bobby nodded and knelt down to pick her up.

Lilith screeched in pain when they tried to move her.

Shane looked her in the eyes. "We're going to carry you to the truck. We'll be as gentle as we can."

"No! No! Please!" she begged.

Shane could see Lilith was using all of her strength to speak.

Bobby lifted her ever so slightly to look behind her back. "It's worse back here. The exit wound, it's bad."

Shane took out his new phone and dialed 911. "All circuits are busy. Your call cannot be completed at this time."

Shane bit his lip to keep from screaming in anger, agony, and frustration. Tears boiled to the surface and trickled down his cheeks. He'd never felt so helpless in his entire life. He looked toward the sky. "God, please, if you don't hate me, please help Lilith. I know I've gone off the path. I'm sorry, but please help us."

He looked down and pulled the hair out of her face.

She batted her eyes once more. "You believe in God?"

"I used to."

She forced a smile. "I guess I'm about to find out."

Shane's concern shifted from her temporal torture to one that would last much longer. "God is real."

She closed her eyes and whispered. "Tell me about Him."

"Well, He's perfect. He's loving. And He forgives us if we ask Him to."

"Okay, how does that work? Do you need a priest or something?"

Shane swallowed hard. "No. Jesus, who is God in the Flesh, came to earth to pay the price for our sins through death on the cross. Since God is perfect, he can't have imperfection in heaven. The Bible says all have sinned and fall short of the glory of God. And it says the wages of sin is death but the gift of God is eternal life. That's mercy and grace. We work hard all day at sinning and we deserve death, all of us. But instead, God gives us eternal life. It's a free gift to those who repent and believe. The Bible says that if you confess with your mouth that Jesus is Lord and believe in your heart that God has raised Him from the dead, you will be saved. Jesus is our Priest. You can just tell him."

Lilith gave a shallow nod. "Jesus, I'm sorry. I haven't been a very good person. I should have taken the time to get to know you. But I always thought it was something I'd do later. Thank you for paying the price for my sins. I'm sure that was tough. I believe in You."

Shane smiled and wiped the tears from his eyes.

"So that's it? I'll go to heaven?" asked Lilith.

He could no longer hold back. Shane began sobbing. Still, he managed to say, "Yes."

Her face softened, no longer contorted by pain. "And you'll come, too? Later, I mean?"

He nodded and kissed her forehead.

She smiled and closed her eyes. "Good." The rising and falling of her chest slowed. Each successive breath became more delicate, until finally, she lay perfectly still, and absolutely quiet.

CHAPTER 17

The Lord is my shepherd; I shall not want. He maketh me to lie down in green pastures: he leadeth me beside the still waters. He restoreth my soul: he leadeth me in the paths of righteousness for his name's sake. Yea, though I walk through the valley of the shadow of death, I will fear no evil: for thou art with me; thy rod and thy staff they comfort me. Thou preparest a table before me in the presence of mine enemies: thou anointest my head with oil; my cup runneth over. Surely goodness and mercy shall follow me all the days of my life: and I will dwell in the house of the Lord for ever.

Psalm 23

Shane felt Bobby put his arm around him.

The giant of a man said tenderly, "Brother, we're going to have to go. We can't hang around here. We can put Lilith in the back seat of your truck. We'll get her cleaned up when we get to your folks' place."

Shane dried his eyes and looked up to see that Bobby had been crying also. He nodded. "Okay."

"You've been shot. I'll take her, if you don't mind."

"Sure." Shane watched Bobby pick up Lilith's corpse so gingerly. He carried her in his arms as easily as Shane might have held a small cat. Her tiny form was swallowed up in Bobby's massive arms.

Bobby's steps were slow and solemn, like a funeral procession. Shane walked ahead and cleared Lilith's luggage from the back seat, tossing it into the bed of the truck. Bobby put her in gently. His eyes looked at Shane compassionately. "You need to take care of that arm."

"My dad will know what to do."

"You could lose a lot of blood in the next hour and a half. Let's tie something on it."

Shane opened his own suitcase and took out one of his plaid shirts. "We can use this. Can you help me put it on?"

Bobby spun the shirt into a long bandage. "You should take off your jacket."

Shane followed his directions. "If only we hadn't

stopped here. Or if I hadn't gone with Derrick earlier. Or if I'd just taken Lilith to Sylva when my dad first invited us. If I'd done anything differently, Lilith would still be alive."

"Don't do that to yourself." Bobby wrapped the shirt around the wound. "Those goons killed Lilith. It's their fault, not yours." He tied it off and tucked in the edges. "My grandma used to drag me to church when I was little. I never heard anything like what you told Lilith. If I had, I'd probably still go to church. What you said was beautiful. If you believe any of it, then you've gotta believe God has a plan, and that He's in control."

Shane sighed. He knew Bobby meant well, but nothing was going to make him feel better; not for a long time. Shane sat the two cartons of beer on the side of the road. His anger and pain were begging him to drink them all right now, but he still had a long road ahead.

***

Two hours later, Shane pulled up the long gravel driveway to his parents' cabin. Darkness fell early in mid-January. Shane's headlights illuminated the path. The porch light was on and Paul came out the door wearing a pistol belt, his .45 Glock 21 in the holster. His welcoming smile quickly gave way to concern when he saw Shane's bloody arm. "What happened?"

"We were attacked in Knoxville. Lilith is dead."

"Oh, Son. I'm so sorry. Let's get you inside and clean you up."

Shane pointed to Bobby who was out of his truck and following him to the house. "This is Bobby. He was Backwoods' head of security. If he hadn't been there, I'd be dead, too."

"Good to meet you," said Paul. "I'm grateful for what you did for Shane."

"Nice to meet you, too, sir. I just wish things could have turned out better."

Shane's mother and sister arrived in the kitchen when he came inside.

Paul looked to the sister, "Angela, I need you to look under the sink in the master bathroom and bring me the medical kit."

She looked worried. "Sure. I'll be right back."

"Tonya," he said to his wife. "We need some old towels and a pot of warm water."

She looked at her son before taking on her tasks. "Are you okay, Shane?"

"I'll be fine," he said, even though he was far from it, his heart aching more than his arm.

"I'll bring in Shane's bag. He'll need some clean clothes once y'all get him fixed up." Bobby walked back out the door.

Once Angela arrived with the medical kit, Paul cut away Shane's shirt. He took a washcloth and dampened it with the warm water Tonya had prepared. He began wiping away the dried blood. "Looks like it went clean through."

Shane winced as his father felt around for a fracture.

Angela's husband, Greg, came into the room. "Can I do anything to help?"

Paul motioned toward the bloody strips of cloth

he'd cut off Shane, "Could you put all this in the trash?"

Greg nodded and retrieved the garbage can.

Paul cleaned the wound with betadine and stitched it up. "If that isn't looking better in a day or two, we'll ask around and find someone to take a look at it. If we take you to the hospital, we'll open up a can of worms with the law. Under normal circumstances, I wouldn't hesitate, but we're operating under a different set of rules."

Shane looked at the stitches which were very good. His father had stitched up his leg once as a teenager after he'd fallen out of a tree and ended up with a nasty laceration. "I was involved in another incident back in Nashville earlier today. So I'd appreciate it if we could keep it discrete."

Paul's look of uneasiness returned. "Do you think they'll come looking for you here?"

"I think Nashville and Davidson County are overwhelmed, and they'll have bigger fish to fry by the time they get caught up. If they ever get caught up."

"Can you tell us what happened?" Tonya used an old scarf to tie a sling for her son's arm.

First, he gave the account of Knoxville, reliving the horror and grief, and telling of Lilith's demise. Next, he briefly described the episode with Derrick and Bridgette south of Nashville.

"We'll get Lilith cleaned up." His mother kissed him. "You go lie down and rest a while. I'd say you've had a rough day, but that would be a vast understatement."

Shane felt terrible, letting everyone else take on

all the responsibilities of carrying for Lilith's final needs, but he was in no shape to help. He'd lost a lot of blood and his body was weak. He decided to take his mother's advice. He walked upstairs and lay down on his old bed, sure that he wouldn't be able to go to sleep.

***

"Shane." His mother shook the bed softly. "I made breakfast. Sausage and white gravy, your favorite."

Shane sat up quickly, but his rapid response was tempered by the sharp pain in his left bicep. The physical pain reminded him of the excruciating emotional anguish of which his slumber had temporarily alleviated him. "What time is it?"

"Eight o'clock." Sunlight crept past the curtains, catching his mother's cheek and illuminating her face like that of an angel.

"Thanks. I'll be down soon." He felt certain that he did not deserve to be this woman's son. The familiar scent of coffee and grease wafted across his nose. He'd not eaten since breakfast on the day prior. The growl in his gut overruled his grief and he forced himself from the warm bed.

Bobby was seated with Shane's family when he arrived at the table. Paul asked God to bless the food, then they all began eating.

"This smells fantastic, Mrs. Black," said Bobby as he ladled gravy over five biscuits.

"You eat all you like," replied Tonya with a smile. "We owe you a debt of great gratitude. If my cooking can satisfy some portion of that, then I'll be pleased."

"Where did you sleep?" Shane spooned some eggs onto his plate.

"Your sister's room." Bobby began eating.

"We're staying in the little house," Angela added.

"We've got that big guest room downstairs." Shane looked at his mother.

His mother and sister exchanged a glance in such a way that told him Lilith's body must be in the guest room. Tonya looked back to her son with sympathy. "Maybe we'll move Bobby down there in a few days."

The rest of the meal was relatively quiet. After they'd finished eating, Paul said, "We'll need to have a funeral for her today. We don't have the kind of resources that a professional undertaker could provide."

Shane looked down at his empty plate. "I understand."

Greg asked, "Should I start digging a grave?"

Paul looked at his son-in-law. "There's a little quiet spot down by the creek. I'll walk you down and show you where it's at."

"I could give you a hand with that," Bobby offered. "If you want."

"Thank you, Bobby." Paul stood up from the table and waved for him to follow. "Let's find you boys some shovels."

Once again, Shane felt useless. His arm was in a sling, so he certainly couldn't dig a grave.

Tonya got up from the table and offered Shane

her hand. "Why don't you come with me?"

He stood, knowing where she would lead him. The two of them walked down the stairs to the guest room.

"Thank you, Mom. I appreciate everything you've done."

Tonya stood by the door. "You're welcome, Son. I'll leave you alone to say goodbye."

Shane stood over the bed where Lilith's body lay. His mother and sister had done a superb job of cleaning her up, putting her in a nice dress, but she did not look like she was sleeping. She looked dead. Even though they'd put a little makeup on her, her skin was pale, almost blue. She'd lost so much blood, she appeared withered. When his father had suggested that they have a service today, he'd thought it felt rushed, but now, he understood. He wanted to touch her, to hold her, but not like this. He chose rather to remember her as she'd been, soft, warm, and alive. Shane stood over her, letting it sink in that she was gone. He cried for a while, then dried his eyes and bid her a final farewell. "Goodbye, baby."

***

Paul made a simple coffin from plywood and two-by-fours. Later that afternoon, they buried Lilith near the creek. Paul read from the Psalms and offered a prayer for Shane's comfort. Then, Shane returned to the house to begin the long process of healing.

CHAPTER 18

And let us consider one another to provoke unto love and to good works: not forsaking the assembling of ourselves together, as the manner of some is; but exhorting one another: and so much the more, as ye see the day approaching.

Hebrews 10:24-25

January 15th, four days after Shane arrived in Sylva, NC.

Shane finished his coffee after breakfast Sunday morning. Everyone else had left the dining room to get ready for church except Shane and his father. With one hand, Shane washed his mug and placed it in the strainer. "Do you think driving to church is the best way to expend gasoline? It's getting close to $100 a gallon."

Paul finished off the coffee pot and began rinsing it out. "This might be the last service we have at Grace Chapel. I'd imagine resources are getting pretty tight for most folks. The Hot Spot has gas, but people don't have much cash after the banks being closed for five days. Even if they did have some money tucked under the mattress, not many can afford $2,000 to fill up their tank.

"I can't imagine people will be showing up to work next week either, unless they can walk to work or take a bike. None of that will matter anymore in a week or two. We'll devolve back into the dark ages. That's why it's so important that we go to church today. I'm going to invite Pastor Joel and a few of the families from church to come live with us."

Shane adjusted his arm sling. "That's why you put those four trailers in the clearing above the front gate?"

"Yep. Got a good deal on them, too."

"Oh yeah?"

Paul sipped from his cup. "Paid five thousand each for them."

"Really? Those are all top-of-the-line travel trailers. Those go for thirty or forty grand. How did you manage that?"

"Storage place out toward Whittier. They rent out space to folks who live up on the mountain where they can't pull a trailer or don't have room to park it. Some of them, their homeowners' association won't let them keep it on the property.

"I went into the office Wednesday morning and gave the clerk $100 to call all the owners. Said I'd pay cash to anyone willing to sell for five thousand. He made less than ten phone calls. I had all four trailers moved in time for lunch."

Shane marveled at his father's shrewd dealings. "You always told me cash would be king in the initial stages of an economic collapse. I guess you were right about that. Who else are you planning to invite to live up there?"

"Dan Ensley, his wife, and boy. We've known Dan for so long, I have to offer him a spot. Plus, as a contractor, he has a valuable skill set for hard times. He hunts, so I figure he'll be a good shooter if it ever comes down to that.

"Fulton and Maggie Farris. They're pretty much our best friends at church. Fulton was an actuary for a big insurance company before he retired. Maggie was a bank manager. We've been talking to them about all of this over the years, so they're somewhat mentally prepared for it. Both of them have learned to shoot, they keep a small garden, and they've allocated part of his savings into precious metals. They'll be an asset."

Shane considered his father's selections. So far, relationship was the determining factor, but all of the proposed guests brought something to the table besides a hungry mouth. "Who will you offer the fourth trailer to?"

Paul took a long drink, finishing his coffee. He looked Shane in the eyes. "The Stanleys."

"The Stanleys?" Shane's brows snapped together

like a broken rubber band which had been stretched too far.

"We've known Will and Julianna for years, Shane. They've been with us at Grace Chapel since Pastor Joel started it. You, of all people, should want them here."

"Oh, yeah? Why is that?"

"The three of you were best friends. You played on the worship team together for years."

Shane turned his back to his father and glared out the window. "That was a long time ago. A lot of water has been under the bridge since then."

Paul put his hand on Shane's shoulder. "Maybe it's time you moved past all of that. Learn to get along, seek reconciliation."

"How can I? After what Will did?" Shane turned back to face his father. "You shouldn't trust him either. He'll do what's best for Will, regardless of who it hurts. Is that the culture you want at your survival retreat?"

Paul washed his cup and put it in the strainer next to the others. "You're right, it's my survival retreat, and it's my decision. However, I do trust Will. What's more, your mother and I love that family. Things are going to get really bad, Son. You've already had a bigger taste of it than most of us. Are you willing to let your anger and pride get in the way of giving their little boy the best chance of living through what's coming?"

Shane felt guilty but doubled down in the face of his wounded heart. "I don't see how he's any of my concern."

Paul looked if he had more to say but remained

quiet for a moment.

Shane drummed his fingers on the counter while shame ate away at his insides.

Finally, Paul asked, "What about Julianna? Would you be okay with her ending up like Lilith? Because that's exactly what will happen unless we intervene."

Shane couldn't believe his father had resorted to such a cheap shot. He turned away before Paul could see his eyes welling up. He spoke softly so as not to betray the emotion cracking in his voice. "I've got to go upstairs and get my Bible for church."

***

The ride to church was cozy, to say the least. Paul's Ram 2500 mega-cab was the roomiest of all the vehicles, but Bobby took up all the passenger space in the front. Shane, his mother, Angela, and Greg had to all compact into the back seat with not an inch to spare.

When the Blacks arrived at the former grocery store transformed into a house of worship, they nearly doubled the morning's attendance.

"Wow, nobody is here!" Tonya exclaimed.

Shane looked around. The pastor, the worship team, and a handful of people were all that he saw. "We had more people than this when we were at the school."

"It's usually about three hundred people. I suppose the bank closure is hurting people faster than I thought." Paul's forehead was heavily lined.

"Who's this scary looking cat up at the front?" Bobby pointed to a man with a full gray beard, tattoos on his knuckles, and a spider web on the back of his hand.

Shane chuckled. "That's Pastor Joel."

"Pastor?" Bobby looked perplexed.

"Yeah. He was in a motorcycle gang before. Did some time for running drugs. Turned his life over while he was in the penitentiary."

"No kidding!"

"Yeah, no kidding." Shane caught himself gazing at Julianna while she walked to the stage to position her microphone. He'd not seen her in nearly seven years. So many absent-minded moments had been spent wondering what she looked like now. Her radiant red hair still contrasted against her milky smooth skin. Her lips were just as voluptuous as they'd ever been, and she seemed to have not aged a minute. Even though his emotions remained raw from losing Lilith, his stomach became a cage of butterflies, swarming as if being chased by a cat. He watched her pull her hair out of her face with one hand and turn toward the crowd.

Shane quickly flicked his eyes to the floor avoiding eye contact with Julianna. In that instant, he knew a few things to be true. Time did not heal all wounds, or if it did, seven years was not a sufficient amount. Also, his father's 24-acre property would be too close for comfort. And finally, he was not over Julianna, not by a long shot.

"Shane Black."

Shane felt a firm squeeze on his shoulder. He turned to see Dan Ensley and his family sitting in the row behind him. He offered his good hand for a shake. "Hey, Dan. Good to see you."

"Where's that pretty little girl you gave the big ring to on TV?"

"She was killed on the way here. Shot." Shane lowered his gaze.

"Oh, no! I'm so sorry to hear it. Is that what happened to your arm?" Dan pointed to the sling.

"Yeah. We were robbed in Knoxville."

Dan shook his head. "I pray God will comfort you."

"Thanks."

"Pretty bad out there, huh?"

"Yeah, total mayhem."

"I've been watching it on the news. I suppose we're blessed to not have it so bad in Sylva."

"It'll be here. No corner of this country will escape what's coming." Shane didn't want to relive all the terror he'd experienced since New Year's Eve, but even this was preferable to having to face Julianna. "I think my dad is going to ask you to move out to the farm with us. You should take him up on the offer."

"We've got a little property. I can handle business if trouble comes my way. I think we'll be alright."

"You have to sleep sometime, Dan. I don't think this is something you'll want to ride out on your own." Shane watched Will kiss his little boy, Cole, on the head and send him to sit next to Dan Ensley's little boy, Scott, who was about the same age.

"I'll listen to what your dad has to say." Dan

patted Shane on the shoulder and sat back in his seat as the music started to play.

After a time of worship, Pastor Joel's message focused on the faith of Job, how he persevered in the face of absolute adversity.

Initially, Shane thought only of the personal application. In a two-week period, he'd lost Lilith, Stan, his career was essentially over, his retirement account worth nothing, his savings account inaccessible, and his 3-million-dollar home was just outside of a war zone. On top of everything else, he wondered if an arrest warrant was lingering about, lying in wait like a lion in the tall grass.

Once Shane had meditated long enough on his own personal pity party, he considered what many others were going through. The single mom he'd been in an accident with on the way home for Christmas, how would she get by in times like these? How would she feed her precious children? He figured her hardship was one that would be cloned by other single mothers, thousands upon thousands of mothers and children who did not have a crazy prepper for a father and a well-stocked survival retreat to call home.

With his good hand, Shane rubbed the residual dust off his old leather-bound Bible and opened it for the first time in a long time. Its spine was broken in, the pages worn. Not one of them lacked an underlined verse. Shane recalled the time in his life when this Book was his most treasured possession. He flipped through the pages with ease and found the Book of Job. As Pastor Joel reached the final point of his sermon, Shane read along quietly, moving his lips and whispering, "Though he slay me, yet will I trust in him."

***

Once the service had ended, Paul quickly made his rounds to issue his invitations. Shane watched as his father spoke with Will Stanley while he packed up his keyboard. He saw Will glance over at him during the conversation and Shane quickly turned away. Shane introduced Bobby and Dan and left the two of them to get acquainted. He listened to his mother and sister's conversation.

"We should invite Mrs. Perkins. She's in her eighties and all alone," said Angela.

Tonya nodded. "I agree. I'll speak to your father about it."

"She can have my room." Angela clasped Greg's arm.

"Okay. Go see if you can get her to hang around for a while. I've got to catch Fulton and Maggie before they get out, then I'll say something to your father about Mrs. Perkins."

His mother and sister parted ways, each to pursue her own mission, and Angela dragging Greg along for the ride.

Shane stood next to Bobby while they waited. Bobby laughed while he watched Cole Stanley run up the aisle to be reunited with his parents who were still on the stage packing their gear.

"What's funny?" Shane cracked a grin, having not experienced a true moment of joy since Lilith's death.

Bobby pointed at the Stanley family. "Neapolitan ice cream."

"I don't get it," said Dan.

"What?" Shane couldn't figure out what the big man was thinking.

He explained his odd comment. He pointed to each of them respectively. "Chocolate, Strawberry, and Vanilla. She's got red hair, he's blonde, and the little boy's hair is as dark as can be."

Dan Ensley acted as if he'd suddenly lost interest in the conversation. "Let me go find my wife before she gets lost." He took his son's hand. "Come on, Scott."

***

An hour later, all of the invitees had arrived at the Blacks' property. Tonya and Angela served fried chicken to all the guests. The cabin's dining area seated only eight, so folks filled a plate and took a seat wherever they could find one. Some on the couch, others at the counter, and still others on the fireplace hearth. After lunch, Paul escorted them all on a brisk tour of the property.

Shane followed along, bundled up warmly in his heavy coat and thermal hat.

When they arrived at the trailers, Paul opened the door to let them in the first of the dwellings. Once inside he said, "I have large camping stoves for the campers, the type used to heat big canvas expedition tents. I can cut and flash openings for the flues, but I'm sure it would come out a lot better if we can talk Dan into taking care of that for us."

Dan Ensley nodded. "It might not pass code, but I can guarantee it won't burn your trailers down if I do it."

"If code enforcement can get out and start writing violations, that's a pretty good sign that things are getting back to normal. At that point we can all go back home," laughed Fulton Ferris.

Paul continued, "Together, we can raise crops, breed animals, secure the property, and fulfill all the necessities of a community. We have fresh water from the spring, fish in the pond, abundant firewood, and a relatively defendable piece of real estate.

"As you can see, this is something I've been anticipating for a long time. I hope you'll all join me. I truly believe that this is our best hope of making it through what's coming."

Cole Stanley held Julianna's leg. He looked at Shane with a bright smile and waved at him.

Awkwardly, Shane returned the grin and gestured back at the lad.

Julianna's eyes flicked from Cole to Shane, then back to her son. She pulled him to the other side, out of Shane's view. "Paul, I really appreciate your offer. But for now, I don't see the need for it."

Will nodded in agreement with his wife. "Things in Sylva aren't all that bad. We'll keep it in mind. Thank you very much for having us out. We're honored that you considered us." Will led his wife and child toward the door. He had to pass by Shane on the way out. He looked at him uncomfortably. "Welcome home, Shane."

"Thanks." Shane forced a smile and waved, not

Dysphoria

knowing how to handle the close proximity to Julianna as she passed by.

Contrived though it was, Julianna's was more of a non-frown than a smile. "Bye," she said concisely.

His expression softened at the sound of her voice. The sweet smell of her perfume lingered behind. "Goodbye." Shane watched her walk out the door.

Pastor Joel was next to speak. He held his wife, Elizabeth's hand firmly. "Before anyone else makes a hasty decision, I want to provide my advice. I think Paul's preparations are nothing short of Solomonesque. He's displayed much consideration and great wisdom. To ignore his plea would be akin to closing your ears to Noah himself as he begs you to enter the ark under dark rain-filled clouds.

"Paul, Elizabeth, and I gladly accept."

"Thank you, Pastor." Paul grinned. "I'm happy to have you aboard the ark."

"You know we're in." Fulton held Maggie's hand.

Dan stood with one arm around his wife, Kari, and the other around his son, Scott. "We're going to take you up on your offer also, Paul. I appreciate it."

Eighty-five-year-old Madeline Perkins looked around at the others. "I'm gonna think on it. Lay it before the Lord in prayer. I'll get back to you tomorrow with my answer. If I come, I'd need to bring Sorghum."

"Who's that?" Paul inquired.

"My cat."

Paul looked at Shane. "Mrs. Perkins will be

upstairs in the main house, across the hall from you. Do you have any objections to her bringing Sorghum?"

"No. I like cats." Shane hoped he'd get along with this particular one.

"And my chickens," she added. "My ducks, too. I don't have no particular affinity to any singular individual foul, mind you, I just like having them around. Ain't got no problem servin' any of 'em up for Sunday dinner neither, especially if they ain't layin'. But I don't know how well they'll get along with your birds, Paul. They's ornery and used to havin' their own space, you see."

"We'll accommodate your birds." Paul nodded. "They'll be a welcome addition to the farm."

***

Monday morning, the farm was a buzz. People coming and going, moving their belongings to the trailers. Dan Ensley took over installing the stoves, although, some of the new residents had brought their own stoves from home, which would be much more efficient than the simple wood-burning camping stoves.

The entire following week was busy with cutting wood, building a separate coop for Mrs. Perkins' hens, and plotting out gardens for the spring. While he was limited on what he could do while his arm was on the mend, Shane welcomed the activity. It served to keep his mind off of Lilith. He still found time to grieve but evaded the dangerous dark hole of depression which threatened to suck him under.

CHAPTER 19

Only the naive inflationists could believe that government could enrich mankind through fiat money.

Ludwig von Mises

January 20th, five days later.

Friday evening, Shane pulled off his sling so he could help his father and Bobby unload the freshly-filled fuel cans from the back of the Ram.

"Put that right back on." Paul pointed at Shane's arm.

Bobby fought a smile and continued unloading the cans into the drive-up basement of the guest cabin.

Shane protested, "I'm not putting any weight on

it. I just need it to steady the five-gallon containers. It feels much better."

"Let me and Bobby take care of offloading the fuel. How about you pull the lids off and put the stabilizer in each can."

Shane pressed his lips together. "Fine."

Bobby said quietly, "Gotta be tough being back home with the folks after all those years."

"Yep." Shane removed the caps from the first few cans.

Paul reminded him, "Use Sea Foam for the diesel. STA-BIL for the gas."

Bobby finished unloading and watched Shane. "At least we didn't have to wait in line."

"Nobody has $3,000 to fill up their tank, at least not in cash." Shane replaced the caps and rocked the containers back and forth to mix the solutions.

Bobby waited for Paul to walk up the drive to the main house. "Nobody except your dad. He's got a pretty deep stash, huh?"

"Probably not after this fuel run. He's trying to get rid of his dollars while anyone will still take them. But at least we'll be able to use the tractor and chainsaws for a while." Shane mixed in the last dose of Sea Foam to ensure the diesel would stay fresh. "Let's get back to the house and get cleaned up. I don't want to miss the president's address."

***

Later that evening, the Blacks' living room was crowded. Everyone in the compound was gathered around the television at the main cabin or the guest cabin.

None of the guests staying in the trailers had televisions. Their only source of electricity was a single heavy-duty extension cord run from the guest cabin to the cleared lot. A power strip in the first trailer allowed a secondary array of extension cords to relay electricity to each of the other three trailers. The residents all abided by the honor system, not to use more than one electric device at a time to keep from overloading the circuit. Non-essentials and high-drain devices were forbidden; no hair dryers, no electric stoves. The residents had scheduled days to use the laundry facilities at the cabins. They also shared the showers.

Shane sat on the landing where the stairs turned to ascend to the second floor. Sitting five steps up from the main floor gave him the perfect view of the television. With his parents, the Farrises, Bobby, Mrs. Perkins, Pastor Joel, and his wife all sharing the living room furniture and counter stools, the landing also offered the most elbow room. It was carpeted, like the stairs from that point upward, and Shane used a pillow to cushion his back against the tongue-and-groove wall.

Tonight's address was from the White House Press Room rather than the Oval Office. The president was introduced by the press secretary. President Donovan spoke into the mic. "Good evening. I've chosen to address you all from this stage because my office can get a little stuffy sometimes. Also, it might place undue credit on the man sitting behind the desk."

Donovan motioned to the entourage of advisors standing at the stage with him. "The people you see with me tonight represent America's best and brightest, especially when it comes to economic policy and crisis management. I'm honored to be part of their team. We've put together a plan which will put our country back on track. We'll be posting a more detailed explanation of the plan on WhiteHouse.gov. But for now, I've chosen the Chairman of the Federal Reserve, Jason Walker to lay out the major points of this plan. Jason has served as the lead architect of this plan and is arguably the smartest person in the room. Additionally, his ability to communicate complex ideas in layman's terms make him the obvious selection to deliver the exciting news we've worked so hard to bring you. Jason." Donovan held out an open hand toward the Fed Chairman and stepped back from the mic.

"Thank you, Mr. President." Apparently having no familiarity with the teleprompter, the man organized his paper notes, pushed his thick glasses up on his nose, and glanced up at the camera with an awkward smile. He had all the hallmarks of a deeply intellectual, socially challenged individual. At 42 years old, Walker was also the youngest Fed Chairman in recent history. "Our current crisis has been absolutely catastrophic, unprecedented, and has gone on longer than any of us ever believed.

"At its core, the crisis is one of confidence. Without a stable currency in which the world and the American people can place their confidence, commerce has ground to a halt.

"Working with international finance leaders at the IMF, our team has developed a replacement currency which will act as a foundation for a new economic platform. Since it is of such dire importance to international trade and the long-term viability of our nation, it is very important that we prove to the world that we are serious about getting our house in order. So, in good faith to the global economic community, we will be phasing in certain austerity measures to moderate government spending. This will no doubt be the least popular aspect to our plan, but trust us when we tell you that it is unavoidable. For decades, the two parties have each protected their own sacred cows when it comes to the Federal Budget. Public welfare programs currently consume nearly 4 trillion annually and military spending is just over 1 trillion. With neither side wanting the tax increases needed to feed these programs, deficit spending has been allowed to grow out of control.

"While we have fought to come up with a plan that will still provide a safety net, particularly to those who have paid into the welfare programs for their entire working lives, the austerity measures are going to hit this portion of our budget the hardest. Likewise, we will also do what is necessary to keep our country safe, but our presence on the world stage will have to be scaled back."

The chairman paused from the monotone delivery of his written speech to look up at the camera for a moment. He attempted another uncomfortable smile, then continued reading. "Now, that we have the bad news out of the way, let's talk about the solution.

"The Federal Reserve Bank will begin to issue its new digital currency at midnight tonight. The new currency will be known as the gold dollar. The gold dollar will be pegged to the price of gold and a weighted basket of international currencies. This currency basket will be represented by supplementary foreign-exchange reserve assets issued by the IMF called Special Drawing Rights.

"The gold dollar will be supervised by a triumvirate of economic authorities, including the Federal Reserve, IMF, and World Bank. This oversight will not only bolster credence among the globe for our fledgling currency, but it will provide guidance to keep us on track in the issuance of the new units. Using the present value of gold and SDRs, the current exchange from old dollars to the new gold dollar is 78 to 1, meaning that for every 78 dollars you had prior to the bank closure, you'll have one new gold dollar when banking resumes.

"We're doing our best to reopen banks on Monday morning so America can get back to business. Once opened, you'll be able to bring in your old paper bills to FDIC member banks and deposit them into an account which will automatically exchange your cash for the new digital currency. As a reminder, no paper or coin will be issued to replace the old dollar. The gold dollar will be 100 percent digital.

"Undoubtedly, we've experienced a significant period of adjustment, particularly as the new gold dollar relates to domestically produced products. The president's team has prepared solutions to mitigate and preempt these issues. The FDA and USDA will be heading up these efforts. I'll turn the platform over to the Secretary of Health and Human Services Patricia Baron to tell you more about that." Chairman Walker once again repositioned his glasses, collected his papers and stepped away from the podium.

A heavy-set woman with a thick jawbone and muscular neck approached the mic. "Thank you, Mr. Chairman. The FDA under Health and Human Services will be working with the USDA. We'll be taking over the pricing for several domestic production industries, particularly those which produce dietary staples such as milk, eggs, peanut butter, cheese, meat, fruit, and vegetables.

"The SEC will be delisting the affected commodities from the regular market until the free market can find an equilibrium for those goods. We'll be making sure prices remain within a range that are affordable to working families yet are still fair to producers. Companies that are not able to adjust to the new mechanism will be nationalized and absorbed by the Federal Government.

"We'll also be issuing ration cards, which will limit the amount of each of these regulated commodities which can be purchased by a household. The USDA will be overseeing the ration program and will be the issuing agency of the cards. They'll utilize IRS filing information to determine the number of people in each household as well as the mailing address for the cards. If any of that information has changed, the IRS will have a special online form in order for you to update your information.

"Both the FDA and USDA will be setting up local offices staffed with enforcement and compliance agents. USDA compliance agents will be working with local IT companies to install card swipe devices for the ration cards at all food retailers. The FDA will be ensuring that commodity prices are adhered to. The set prices will be for generic goods. Brands will be allowed up to a 20 percent discretionary premium over the set generic price.

"In closing, we recognize that the new plan is not perfect, but it is what we have to work with. Hopefully, everyone will cooperate and commerce will soon begin to flow smoothly." The grisly woman stepped back. "Mr. President."

Donovan once again stepped to the mic. "Thank you, Pat. And thank you, America. I look forward to serving you as president through this storm and into the next phase of our country. One that will be marked by prosperity, cooperation, and the American spirit."

Shane ran his hand through his thick dark hair. "What was that bit about price controls until the free market can find equilibrium? Are they suggesting we rely on command-and-control communism until the invisible hand of capitalism can take over? Aren't those two systems mutually exclusive?"

Paul Black looked over the back of the sofa. "I'm as confused about that as you are. That's the conundrum of having your proverbial cake and eating it, too."

Pastor Joel shook his head. "I feel duped. I voted for Donovan. Not that I had any illusion about him having an above average understanding of freedom. He certainly wasn't my first choice in the Republican primaries. But I never expected anything like this out of him."

Shane's mother put her hand on the pastor's shoulder. "We all did. Whatever crime against the Constitution Donovan is committing, I'm still convinced the other one would have done something worse."

Fulton Farris gestured toward the television. "At least they took one piece of advice from Paul's playbook. They're backing the new currency with gold."

Paul shook his head. "They're pegging it to gold. Big difference. But I assume that was the inference they were looking for by calling it the gold dollar. From what I heard Walker say, this is just another fiat currency."

Shane added from the staircase landing, "Lipstick on a pig."

"That's right, Son." Paul turned to face Shane.

Maggie Farris held her palms up. "How do they expect us to believe that they have the competence to pull any of this off in the first place? Do they think we've forgotten about the government healthcare exchange launch fiasco? They'd had months to build that system out. Now we're supposed to believe these geniuses can cobble together a complete overhaul of the economy by Monday morning?"

"You're right," said Elizabeth Hayes. "That's why Joel and I decided to take Paul up on his offer to come stay here."

Bobby sat at one of the barstools at the counter. "Mr. Black, what do you make of them issuing the new currency only in digital form? Do you suppose that's because it would take too long and be too expensive to issue paper currency?"

Paul pointed to his son. "Shane's heard me preach on this enough. I want to see if he can answer it."

Shane felt like a high school student who'd just been called on. Nevertheless, his father's assumption was correct. He'd been educated by the man on the effects of deficit spending and monetary creation since he was old enough to count. But, to him, it had all seemed like a prophecy that would never come true, at least not in his lifetime. For that reason, Shane had ventured off the path of prudence in his own life. Yet here it was, his father's most apocalyptic visions being fulfilled in living color before his very eyes. Fortunately for Shane, his father had not allowed complacency to creep in during the years ruled by a mirage of economic prosperity. Shane owed his father the respect of showing that he still retained the knowledge imparted to him.

He considered the question and formulated his answer. "Time and expense to print new currency is certainly an issue, but it's probably not the biggest factor. In Venezuela, for example, the government had an official exchange rate, which artificially inflated the value of the bolivar. However, the black-market exchange rate more closely reflected the actual value of the failed currency. I can't remember exactly, but the official rate was something like 200 thousand bolivars to 1 US dollar. The black market, however, would give you 4 million bolivars for a dollar. That fact alone discredited the official rate.

"Besides that, anytime you have a failed currency, the country undergoes capital flight. Argentineans in 2001, and Russians in the 90s, both tried to get as much money as they could out of the country when it became obvious that their currencies were collapsing. Before them, in the 20s and 30s, Germans who understood what was happening at least tried to get their money out of marks and into francs, if not out of the country altogether.

"If Donovan wants us to all stick together and cooperate, he can't have everyone with more than a thousand dollars jumping ship and looking for greener grass. Keeping the currency electronic makes it much easier to track and control. An economic Hotel California, I guess." Shane looked to his father as if to ask, *how did I do?*

Paul's proud smile spoke louder than words. "Good answer, Son."

CHAPTER 20

Then the Gods of the Market tumbled, and their smooth-tongued wizards withdrew
And the hearts of the meanest were humbled and began to believe it was true
That All is not Gold that Glitters, and Two and Two make Four
And the Gods of the Copybook Headings limped up to explain it once more.

As it will be in the future, it was at the birth of Man
There are only four things certain since Social Progress began.
That the Dog returns to his Vomit and the Sow returns to her Mire,
And the burnt Fool's bandaged finger goes

wabbling back to the Fire;

And that after this is accomplished, and the brave new world begins
When all men are paid for existing and no man must pay for his sins,
As surely as Water will wet us, as surely as Fire will burn,
The Gods of the Copybook Headings with terror and slaughter return!

Excerpt from Gods of the Copybook Headings—Rudyard Kipling

January 23rd, three days after the introduction of the new gold dollar.

Shane put on his pistol belt Monday evening. Paul had instituted a condition-orange security protocol for the compound after news broadcasts had covered riots in Knoxville, Asheville, and Greenville. The government's promise of opening banks by Monday morning had failed, leaving desperate people enraged by yet another let down by the government they'd been taught to trust more than God Himself.

A knock came to his bedroom door. "You ready?"

Shane opened the door to Bobby towering above him. He zipped up his thick winter coat and stuck his pistol in the holster. "Let's go."

"No sling?"

"It's been two weeks. I need to move it around anyway. We're just walking around the property. It's not like I'm doing any heavy lifting."

"Okay, but for the record, if your dad asked, I recommended that you put it on."

"Duly noted. Come on." Shane led the way down the stairs.

The two men followed a trail which led up the mountain behind the main house and circled around the property. They walked slowly, keeping a diligent eye, but expecting to see nothing. Trouble was still far from them, but Shane trusted his father when he suggested it would soon be upon them. Shane and Bobby talked about everything. The discussed the glory days that were long gone, reminiscing about the good times and bad which they'd shared. With Lilith gone, Bobby was Shane's only connection to a life which no longer existed.

Shane's phone buzzed in his pocket. He took it out. "It's Derrick."

"No kidding. Put it on speaker," suggested Bobby.

"Derrick, hey, I'm here with Bobby."

"Hey, guys. Good to hear you're both doing okay. Bridgette told me to tell you that she thinks about you every day. We're both so sorry about what happened to Lilith."

Shane looked at the forest floor coated with leaves, last season's graveyard that was yet to be replaced by life and vigor. "I miss her. I suppose I always will. How's the neighborhood?"

"That's what I was calling you about. The riots are spreading. Things seemed to calm down for a while, but this morning, when the banks didn't open, people started getting crazy again. Grocery stores around here haven't been open since last week. They ran out of stock pretty quickly once the banks and credit card companies shut down. People are getting desperate."

Shane hated to hear Derrick sounding so frantic. He wished he could invite him to come to Sylva but leave Bridgette behind. He knew Derrick would never do such a thing. He couldn't blame him. "Why don't you two come on down to my dad's? He's got an extra trailer where you can stay."

"Thanks for the offer. If we could scavenge the gas to do it, I'd take you up on it. Both our vehicles have been siphoned. I doubt we could get more than a few miles."

"Sorry to hear that."

"But I was wondering if you'd mind letting us stay at your house. Just being an extra two miles from downtown would make us feel so much better."

Shane answered. "Yeah, absolutely. You've still got a key, right?"

"Yeah. Buddy, I sure appreciate this."

"Of course," said Shane. "Most of that extra food I bought should be there. Unless someone has broken in and stolen it. Help yourself to it."

"You don't know how much that means to us. We're out of everything. I had ketchup and mayonnaise for dinner last night."

Shane wrinkled his forehead. "You mean like on

a sandwich?"

"Ha. I wish. I mean ketchup straight out of the bottle and scooping mayonnaise out of the jar with a soup spoon."

"Brother, you should have called before. What's mine is yours."

"Thanks. I didn't want to bother you with our problems. You have enough to deal with after losing Lilith."

"No worries at all. Be safe."

"I will. You and Bobby take care of each other. Thanks again." Derrick ended the call.

Bobby's face looked worried. "I sure appreciate you bringing me here. I'd be dealing with all that if I were still in Nashville."

"I'm glad you're here. My dad is, too. He likes having you around."

"I'll always do my part. You can count on that."

"I know." Shane patted Bobby on the arm and continued the patrol.

***

Shane's arm continued to heal throughout the week. Paul kept him occupied by assigning him to guard patrol. Shane looked forward to being able to cut wood and do other chores once he was fully healed.

Friday afternoon, Shane knocked on Dan Ensley's trailer door.

Seven-year-old Scott answered. "Hey, Shane."

"Hey, buddy. Is your dad home?"

"No. He's at Greg's, watching the news. Do you

think Cole is going to move here?"

"I don't know, buddy. That's up to his mom and dad. I guess you'd like to have someone your age nearby, wouldn't you?"

The young boy shrugged, as if unwilling to admit his need for comradery.

Shane messed up Scott's hair. "We've got a trailer all set up for him if his family decides to come."

"Okay. Are you going on patrol with my dad?"

"Yes, sir."

"I can come if you need me."

Kari Ensley came to the door. "You most certainly cannot."

"Why not? I can shoot."

"Hi, Shane." Kari's mouth set in a hard line. "I have his father to thank for that one. We'd decided that Scott wouldn't get his first rifle until he was ten. But then all of this happened and Dan was afraid we'd never get another chance to buy him one. I was under the impression that we were going to keep the gun hidden until his tenth birthday." Her eyebrows raised and she put her hand on her hip. "However, Dan had other plans."

Shane was eager to get away from the vexed spouse. "Scott, you best hang around here and watch out for your mama while your dad's away."

"Okay. I guess I better," replied the duty-burdened youth. "Come on, mama. We need to keep the doors closed."

Kari mouthed the word, "Thanks," and closed the door as she'd been instructed.

Shane shook his head and followed the hill down

to the guest cabin. He arrived and rapped gently on the wooden door.

Angela answered. "Hey, Shane. Come on in."

Shane entered and saw Dan and Greg sitting on the rustic log, white cedar futon, watching the news. "What's happening?"

"World is going to the devil, that's what." Dan glanced back only for a second.

Shane watched the video of a grocery store being looted by what seemed to be hundreds of people. They had carts filled, or simply carried as much as they could in their arms. With their booty in tow, they ran past managers and workers who pleaded with them to stop. "Where is that?"

"That's in Jacksonville, Florida, but they've been showing the same scenes all over the country," Greg answered.

"You just missed the looting in Charlotte. They showed some manager hanging on to some gal for dear life. She was about twice his size. She dragged him clear across the parking lot to the car, then kicked him off like a clump of dirt on her shoe." Dan sounded amused.

"What started all of this?" Shane stood behind the futon looking on at the melee.

Greg kept his attention on the television. "The banks finally opened yesterday, but if a person didn't have money in the bank before the closures, they still have nothing now. Credit cards aren't working. The credit companies have closed most people's accounts or dropped their limit to their outstanding balance. They're making them reapply to prove they have a way to pay off their balances."

Angela sat at the counter on the matching rustic log swivel stool. "Even if people had money, at that exchange rate, someone with $1,000 now has like $13 in the new gold dollars. The new FDA mandatory price caps are out, but most grocery stores haven't adjusted yet. No enforcement agencies are set up yet, except for one in Washington D.C., which is basically just a prototype.

The big grocery chains are saying they need time to revamp their systems. They've all pledged to be up with the new standards when the ration cards and the swipe machines are operational, but who knows when that will be?"

Shane nodded. "It all sounded so smooth at the press conference. Who would have thought this grand government scheme would fail so miserably?"

Angela, Greg, and Dan all raised their hands.

"It was a rhetorical question." Shane grinned. "Dan, we better get going before my dad notices no one is on patrol."

Dan stood up from the futon. "I'm coming." He grabbed his AR-15 and followed Shane out the door.

Shane waved to his sister and brother-in-law. "See you later. Greg, make sure you keep your radio and rifle nearby. You and Bobby are on call."

Greg held up his walkie talkie to show he was already on it. "Stay warm out there. It's cold."

Once outside, Shane led the way. "Let's do a perimeter sweep. Going up the hill will warm us up."

"Sounds like a plan."

"Heard you got in hot water over buying a rifle for Scott."

"Yeah. It was the shootin' part she got steamed over. But she didn't want to come out here to live neither. I want the boy to learn how to use a gun before game day. The way things are lookin', we might not have much time. My job as a husband is to keep them safe first. After that, we can worry about gettin' 'em comfortable. But Kari's a good woman. She knows it's all for the best. I don't imagine any mama wants to think about her little ones havin' to shoot to stay alive."

"That's understandable." Shane took deep breaths as they marched up the steep hill. "For what it's worth, I think you're doing the right thing."

"We've been using your little shooting range down by the creek. Figured you wouldn't mind."

"Not at all. I set it up because I haven't had time to do much shooting in the past few years. Needed to brush up and knock the dust off my rifle. But it's there for anyone who wants to use it."

"How's that coming along? The brushin' up, I mean."

Shane grinned. "Just like riding a bike. I can keep a grouping as tight as any of you mountain boys around here."

***

Later that evening, Shane and his family sat around the fireplace in the living room.

Bobby asked, "How long did it take you to build

the main cabin?"

"Longer than we thought," Paul seemed to reminisce. "We had more than our share of setbacks. Folks in the mountains don't move as fast as they do in the city. Sometimes, that's a good thing, but when you're trying to build a house, it can be frustrating. We had a learning curve in mountain living, too."

"Like what?" Greg inquired.

"Flying squirrels for one."

"Is he joking?" Bobby turned to Shane.

"I wish he were." Shane shook his head. "Those things get between the cathedral ceiling and the roof. They're nocturnal, so they scratch all night. They've kept me up until morning more times than I can count."

Paul chuckled. "Reminds me of a funny story. Tonya has often brought home some peculiar tasting food items, particularly her teas. The stranger the taste, the more she likes it. If it's got a bitter twinge, notes of licorice, that's right up her alley. What's the one that smells like feet, honey?"

With her arms crossed, Tonya shook her head disapprovingly. "Valerian, but it's not that bad."

Paul kept talking. "Anyway, I came in one evening and helped myself to a kettle she had steeping on the stove. She went to bed and forgot all about it, as she does from time to time. This was the worst tasting concoction I'd ever tasted. But, I'd sort of gotten used to foul-smelling tea. I went ahead and finished my cup but then proceeded to wash out the pot."

Bobby was already shaking his head and

covering his mouth.

Paul nodded affirmatively. "One of them rascals had crawled in the teapot and died!"

Greg threw his hands in the air. "That's the worst story I've ever heard."

"That's why your wife doesn't drink tea to this day." Paul pointed to Greg.

"Nope. I'm done with it." Angela shook her head adamantly.

Shane got out of his chair and walked to the window. "Someone is speeding up the drive."

Pastor Joel's voice came over the radio. "This is patrol. I'm going to need back up at the gate. Anyone that can hear me, get on down here."

"Everyone, make sure you've got a gun. Hopefully, it's someone we know, but if not, let's be ready for it." Paul made his way to the master bedroom.

Shane grabbed his rifle and headed for the door.

CHAPTER 21

And David's anger was greatly kindled against the man; and he said to Nathan, As the Lord liveth, the man that hath done this thing shall surely die: and he shall restore the lamb fourfold, because he did this thing, and because he had no pity. And Nathan said to David, Thou art the man. Thus saith the Lord God of Israel, I anointed thee king over Israel, and I delivered thee out of the hand of Saul.

2 Samuel 12:5-7

Shane, Bobby, Greg, and Paul hurried down the drive to the front gate. Shane could see Pastor Joel standing near the vehicle, embracing someone. Fulton Farris was removing the lock and opening the gate. Shane held up his radio. "What's going on down there?"

Fulton replied. "It's Julianna. Something's happened to Cole."

Shane felt terrible for her.

Paul lifted his radio. "Pastor Joel, bring her on up to the main cabin. Fulton, you watch the gate."

"Roger." Fulton could be seen in the distance waiting for Pastor Joel to drive Julianna up the hill.

"Come on, boys. Let's get back to the house." Paul motioned for his team to follow him up the drive.

Pastor Joel drove Julianna to the front door. He escorted her inside. She cried hysterically.

Mrs. Perkins stroked Julianna's hair. "Calm down, child."

"Just tell us what happened," Paul said softly.

Julianna took a glass of water from Tonya. She took a sip and tried to speak in between double breaths which bordered on convulsions. We . . . we . . . we . . . tried to, go . . . to . . . the store. We . . . hadn't been since before the . . ."

"Focus on your breathing," Angela coached. "Three deep breaths in, hold it, three slow breaths out."

Julianna followed Angela's example and soon had her respiratory system under control. "We were able to buy a few items from Publix. They didn't have much. Inside was chaos. When we left, some guy bumped into me and knocked me down. Another guy grabbed our cart and took off running.

Will chased after the man with the cart, then another one grabbed my purse and ran. I turned for one second to yell at the guy . . ." She broke down once again into uncontrollable sobs. "When I looked back, Cole was gone. I heard him screaming for me while they shoved him in a van. I ran as fast as I could . . ." Julianna wailed into Pastor Joel's shoulder. "He's gone!"

Paul put his hand on her back. "Shhhhh. We'll get Cole back. I promise."

She looked up from Pastor Joel's arm. "You can't promise that."

"I can promise that I'll do everything in my power. Where's Will?"

"At home. In case Cole comes there or they send a ransom note."

"Good." Paul tried to comfort her, rubbing her back. "Did you call the police?"

"Yes, but we couldn't get through. 911 is overloaded."

Paul pointed to Greg. "Try calling the Sheriff's Department. Look up the direct line. We might have a better chance that way than getting routed through 911."

Greg took out his phone and stepped into the hallway.

Elizabeth Hayes asked Julianna, "Does Cole know his address?"

"Yes, and he knows my phone number."

"Good," replied the pastor's wife.

"I begged God all the way here to bring Cole back. I begged Him that it's just a kidnapping and not something worse. But we don't have anything to pay a ransom with." She returned to her uncontrollable sobbing. "I don't know why they would kidnap Cole."

"Could be just because they saw you had enough resources to buy groceries. People are desperate right now," Shane said.

"But this was organized. This was planned out and had several people doing different things to distract us."

Pastor Joel held her firmly. "The Surenos 13 gang has been in Knoxville for a while. Kidnapping is part of their MO. They may be using the crisis to expand their influence. Or it could be another gang adapting their tactics in the face of hard times. But it sounds like a kidnapping to me."

"Don't worry about resources. I'll make sure you have whatever you need to get Cole back." Paul put his hand on her shoulder once more. "Pastor Joel, if you can hold down the fort here, I'll go stay with Will. He's probably losing his mind sitting in that house all alone. He might need back up, too." Paul put on his coat and grabbed his rifle.

"I'll take care of things here," said the pastor.

***

The hours passed slowly. Everyone waited in deep anticipation for news about Cole. Julianna sat on the couch next to Tonya, staring blankly at the flickering fire. Greg and Angela had long since left to go to bed. Likewise, Elizabeth Hayes, Bobby, and Mrs. Perkins had all turned in hours ago. Only Shane, Tonya, and Pastor Joel stayed to keep the vigil with Julianna.

Shane wished so badly that he could hold her, make her feel better, bring back Cole. He could do none of those things. It tortured his soul to have her so near yet know she was so far from ever being his. Yet, it was a punishment he felt he deserved, and that made it somehow bearable. Seeing her in pain, worrying about her son, that was a penalty no one earned; this he could not withstand.

Just before 6:00 AM, Julianna's phone buzzed. She fumbled to pick it up from the coffee table. Shane sprung from his seat on the hearth. He'd almost fallen asleep.

Julianna read the text. "We want 1K in gold dollar. You can bring in gold, silver, or diamond. If you can't get you can buy diamond online and pay for rush delivery. Probably two day. Make sure is GIA certify. Text back this number when you have ransom ready. If you play game or call police, boy will die."

She looked up mournfully. "That's like eighty thousand dollars in old money. And it might as well be a million. We don't have anything worth that much except our house. No one is going to buy a house with everything that's going on. I'm sure a bank isn't going to lend on it either." Julianna's face contorted into woe and she began crying softly.

Shane sat on the coffee table, wanting to keep his distance. "I think I have something they'll take."

She looked up hopelessly as if Shane couldn't possibly deliver on such an absurd offer. "What?"

"I have Lilith's ring. I paid well over a hundred thousand for it."

"Is it GIA certified?"

"Yeah."

"Do you have the paperwork on it?" Her expression changed to one of hope.

"No. But it has a serial number engraved on it. If they know what they're doing, they can look it up. From the sound of things, this isn't the first time they've done something like this."

"And you don't mind giving it to me? We could never pay you back."

"Of course I don't mind. I'll go get it." Shane took out his phone and called his dad on the way upstairs to get the ring. "Hey, Dad. They contacted Julianna." He described the ransom request and told Paul about the ring. "Do you have a loupe? I'll never be able to see the serial number without it."

"Yeah, on top of the safe in my bedroom. I'll bring Will to the house. Go ahead and see if they'll accept the diamond." Paul ended the call.

Shane went to his closet and retrieved Lilith's jewelry box. He took out the ring which reminded him of his loss. Not just Lilith, but everything. His old life, his home, the band, his comfortable lifestyle. It was all gone except this small sparkling stone and a few other lingering trinkets. "I don't know what else this will ever be good for. Might as well put it to good use."

Shane hurried down the stairs to fetch his father's loupe, then returned to the living room. He turned on the light and studied the girdle of the diamond for several minutes looking for the microscopic engraving. "Okay, I found it. Julianna, type these numbers into your phone." Shane read out the serial number.

Next, he placed the ring on the table. "Send them a picture of the ring, then give them the report number."

Julianna followed his directions. "Done. Now what?"

Pastor Joel said, "Let's give them time to look it up."

Julianna glanced up at Shane but quickly turned away. She looked at him once more. "Thank you for this."

"I'm glad I could do it."

She picked up the ring while she waited for a response. "I saw you give this to Lilith, right before the riots started in New York."

Shane wished it had been Julianna on the stage with him that night, but knew she'd have been miserable. "Yeah, that was a rough night." He remembered seeing Stan die so he and Lilith could escape.

Julianna's phone buzzed. She read the text from the kidnappers. "Meet by raft center on 23 at river. One hour. Come alone or boy die."

"It's 6:15 right now. So that's 7:15" Tonya checked the time on her phone.

"That part about you going alone ain't gonna happen." Pastor Joel picked up his pistol from the coffee table and placed it in his holster. "Shane, you gear up and be ready to move out when Will and your dad get here. I know exactly where the rafting center is. We'll have to leave early so we can come in the back way without being spotted. We'll come up Sutton Branch to Macktown Gap Road."

Shane nodded. "I'll wake Bobby. We'll be ready when Dad gets here."

Ten minutes later, Will stormed into the living room followed by Paul. "What's the plan?" Will looked enraged.

Pastor Joel replied, "They've asked Julianna to make the trade, and they've demanded that she come alone."

"The police are out of this?" Will asked.

"So far," said Paul. "Greg called the Sheriff's Department. Took him a while to get through. When he finally did, they said to call back when we heard from the kidnappers. Sounds like they're overwhelmed and understaffed."

"What if they try to take Julianna or what if Cole isn't with them when she gives them the diamond?" Will's face showed the aggravation and rage of a distressed father.

"That's why we'll be there. We'll put snipers up in the trees across the road, and we'll have two trucks ready to respond from either direction." The pastor put his hand on Will's shoulder. "If all goes as planned, we give them the diamond and bring Cole home. It's not worth it to endanger him or anyone else for a shiny rock."

Will looked around the room. "Okay. Who are you going to use as snipers?"

Paul replied, "You still deer hunt every season. I suppose your aim is as good as ever. Shane will be the second shooter. Bobby will ride with me. Pastor Joel will drive Shane's truck. That leaves Greg, Fulton, and Dan to hold down the fort here."

"What should I do?" Tonya asked.

"Pray," answered Pastor Joel.

"Julianna, let's get your phone, my phone, Will's, and Pastor Joel's on a four-way call. Turn your volume all the way down and black out your screen. Just keep the phone in your pocket and we'll be able to hear what's going on." Paul dialed her number.

She took out her phone while Paul set up the call. "What if they check my phone?"

"Then Shane and Will can take them out. We'll be there before they even know what's happening." Paul slung his AR-15 over his shoulder. "Julianna, make sure you have that ring and that your phone stays on. Let us worry about everything else."

She seemed unable to smile, yet her eyes conveyed the gratitude in her heart. "Okay. Thank you all so much for your help. I don't know what we would have done without you." Her eyes flicked to Shane but quickly turned away.

"Let's make sure everyone has a gun and roll out." Paul waved his hands like a general motivating his troops.

***

Pastor Joel drove Shane's truck. Since Will was the nervous father, Shane let him ride up front. It seemed a small thing against the horror Will and Julianna were going through, but he was happy to not have to sit next to Will for the ride over. Nevertheless, they'd soon be side by side in the woods with a thorny uneasiness loitering between them.

Pastor Joel raced up Sutton Branch Road. "I'll turn off Macktown Gap right before the rafting center. That road will put you right beside the old folks' home on the hill overlooking the rafting center. You should be able to slip across their access road then work your way down the hill until you have a good shot."

"I think I know where you're talking about," said Shane.

Minutes later, Pastor Joel rolled to a stop. "This is as far as I go. Just through those trees is the retirement home. You boys go with God. Hopefully, this will all work out, and we won't have to kill anyone. But if you do, shoot straight and shoot to kill. This is to bring Cole home. God expects no less of you."

Shane and Will hurried out of the truck without a word. They hustled through the trees and quietly down the access road. Shane led the way into the brush to make their descent down the steep hill.

Shane attempted to break the stilted tension between them. "Old Brer Rabbit himself wouldn't want to be in a thicket with this many briars."

Will picked past the brambles trying not to get caught up in them. "Yeah."

Shane lifted his feet high, stepping past a long wiry vine laced with thorns. He steadied himself on a sapling as he worked his way lower down the sheer cliff. Will followed in his tracks.

"I think this is our spot. It's flat and it offers a good vantage point." Shane pointed to the rafting center below.

"No shortage of briars." Will pulled back a

barbed branch which had caught on his pant leg. "But everything else around here looks about the same. I guess this will have to do."

Shane and Will slowly cleared out a small nest from which to watch the action below.

"Here she comes." Shane pointed out Julianna's car as it pulled into the parking lot near the rushing white water of the Tuckasegee River.

Will took out his phone, checked to make sure it was muted and watched through his scope. The two men waited quietly for what seemed like forever. Will broke the silence. "We appreciate you putting up that diamond so we can bring Cole home."

"I'm happy to be able to do it. That ring is essentially what got Lilith killed. A part of me is glad to see it go."

"I'm not sure what your interpretation of the facts are surrounding me and Julianna getting married so soon after you two split up, but just as a reminder, things aren't always what they seem."

"What?" Shane had not asked for an explanation. It had been years, and he was perfectly content to let sleeping dogs lie. But since he'd brought it up, this was as good of a time as any for Shane to speak his mind. "I don't know what other conclusion I could reach. I turned my back for five minutes and you two were married. Obviously, something was already going on while I was still here. But Julianna is her own person; capable of making her own choices."

Will snorted and shook his head. "You really have no idea, do you?"

"About what?" Shane had to fight to keep his eye

on the scope.

"As I said, things aren't always what they seem. Remember the story in the Bible about King David. Nathan, the prophet, tells David a story about a rich man who took the one little ewe lamb of a poor man. David is quick to condemn the man to death. Then, Nathan reveals that the story was really about how he'd murdered Uriah and committed adultery with Bathsheba. All the while David was ready to put the rich man to death, it was really him who was guilty."

Shane felt even more confused. "Listen, all that is in the past. You and Julianna are husband and wife. I respect that. I would never try to do anything to come between you two, and I'm sure she would be no part of it anyway. You don't have anything to worry about."

Will kept a steady eye on his scope. "I appreciate your assurance on that matter, but that's not what I'm talking about."

Shane felt complete bewilderment. "Then what was that story all about?"

"At some point, you and Julianna need to sit down and have a talk." Will held his finger to his mouth. "Here they come."

Shane quickly put the baffling conversation out of his mind and focused on the white van pulling into the parking lot. He watched Julianna exit her vehicle with her hands up.

A man got out of the passenger's side of the van and approached her. His voice came over Will's phone. "You bring it?"

"Yes."

Shane could see her remove the ring from her pocket.

The man took it and inspected the diamond with a loupe. "Okay. Looks good. We gonna call you later."

"Call me later? Where's my son? You said you'd bring Cole! I want to see him now!"

"You gonna see him. Just relax."

"Are you going to give him to me now?"

"In a little while."

Paul's voice came over Will's phone. "If you have a clear shot, take him now. They're messing with us."

"On one." Shane tensed up. "I'll go for the chest, you aim for his head. Three, two, one . . ."

POW! POW! Shane and Will's rifles echoed across the river in unison. The man fell to the ground. The driver of the van spun in the gravel, kicking rocks into the air until the vehicle gained enough traction to climb the hill to the road.

Shane watched from above, unable to affect the events playing out below. Julianna stood frozen by the man's corpse, his blood splattered on her coat. Pastor Joel careened toward the van scrambling to escape the parking lot.

BAM! Pastor Joel slammed into the front of the van, sending it spinning and rolling on its side back toward the river.

"Let's go!" Shane pulled the sleeve of Will's jacket. "We need to get down there!"

The two of them dashed like a pair of whitetail bucks back up the cliff to the road and then sprinted down to the riverbank.

They arrived winded, both men's chests heaving. Will ran to the van. "Was Cole in there?"

"Afraid, not," Paul said. "But we got the driver. He'll tell us what we need to know."

Bobby held the driver by the back of his jacket. He shook him around like a rag doll. "Come on. Let's get you taped up before you hurt yourself."

Julianna stood with her mouth hanging open in disbelief. "Why wouldn't they just bring him?"

Pastor Joel had minor abrasions from the airbag on his face. "Maybe they thought we came up with the ransom a little too easily. Probably planning on milking us for a little more. Will, why don't you drive Julianna back to the house? We'll mop up here."

Once Will and Julianna had left, Pastor Joel looked at the smashed-in grill of Shane's truck. "You're gonna need a new airbag."

"Yeah." Shane walked over to the dead man. He pulled the diamond from his hand. The thing seemed to be cursed, but he figured it may still have some use before everything was said and done.

CHAPTER 22

Wherefore if thy hand or thy foot offend thee, cut them off, and cast them from thee: it is better for thee to enter into life halt or maimed, rather than having two hands or two feet to be cast into everlasting fire.

Matthew 18:8

Once the teams arrived back at the Blacks' compound, Shane and Bobby dragged the man into the basement area beneath the little cabin. The man's hands and feet were well secured with duct tape. Will rushed down the road from the main cabin to join them. Paul turned on a single work light clamped to the floor joist overhead. Pastor Joel closed the door behind them.

Will drew his pistol and stuck it in the man's mouth. "Tell me where he is, or I'll blow your head off!"

Pastor Joel gingerly pulled Will's hand away from the man and relieved him of his pistol. "Will, if he's dead, your hopes of ever seeing Cole again die with him."

Paul led Will away from the hostage. "Bobby, why don't you take Will for a walk down by the creek?"

"Sure." Standing hunched over, the big man was obviously uncomfortable in an area with such low ceilings. "Come on, Will." Bobby's massive arm gently wrapped around Will and escorted him out the door.

"Have you got a deer-skinning kit?" Pastor Joel asked.

"I do. It's up at the house." Paul nodded.

"One of those fine medical kits you have might come in handy also. And if you have enough antibiotics to spare, he's gonna need them."

"I'll run and get them." Paul left the musty cellar.

Shane closed the door behind his father.

Pastor Joel pointed at the pair of sawhorses. "Let put that sheet of plywood up on those. We'll make us a work table."

"Is this going to get messy?" Shane asked.

"Probably so." Pastor Joel took off his heavy coat.

"We've got a roll of tarp over in the corner. Should we put that down before we set up the table?"

"Might not be a bad idea." Pastor Joel walked with Shane to get the tarp.

"What are you going to do to me?" The man's eyes followed Shane and Pastor Joel's every move.

Pastor Joel placed one sawhorse in position while Shane situated the other. Pastor Joel assisted him in lifting the plywood up onto the supports. "I'm gonna cut your leg off."

With his voice somewhere between a cry and a scream, the man asked, "Why? Why would you do that?"

"So when I ask you where that little boy is, you'll know I'm serious when I threaten to cut off the other one." The pastor looked at him almost as if it were a silly question.

"But I'll tell you right now! You don't have to do that!"

The pastor motioned for Shane to grab the man's shoulders while he lifted the legs. "I'm sure you would, but how would I know you're telling the truth? Once you've been liberated of that leg, you'll be more motivated, to be honest. Right now, it's just the fear talking. You don't really know how bad it's gonna hurt. It's all abstract. Thirty minutes from now . . ." Pastor Joel gripped the man by the jaw and set his face close to that of his captive. "You're going to have an intimate knowledge of what pain and agony are all about."

Paul returned with the skinning kit and the first aid pouch. He handed them to Pastor Joel. Apprehension filled his eyes but he said nothing.

"Can I speak to you a minute, Pastor?" Shane asked.

"Sure."

"Outside?"

Pastor Joel turned to Paul. "Can you keep an eye on our friend?"

"I'll watch him."

Shane and Pastor Joel stepped out the large swinging garage door. "You're not going to actually cut his leg off, are you? We're just trying to scare him, right?"

"I'm gonna cut it off."

"But why? He said he'd tell us where they're holding Cole. What about all those sermons about love and mercy?" Shane looked at the man's tattooed knuckles. "Have you forgotten where God found you?"

"Not at all." Pastor Joel's voice was calm and even. He put his hand on Shane's shoulder. "This is the most loving, merciful thing I know to do. That man in there is the worst of the worst. Kidnapping is an excessively violent crime. Even if we manage to get Cole back, that boy is probably going to have nightmares for the rest of his life.

"Society has collapsed. We don't have a system to deal with people like that monster in there. Our two choices are kill him or set him free. We certainly can't afford to build a prison, and we couldn't do that to Cole anyhow. Imagine that poor boy knowing his captor was on the same property. He'd never sleep again.

"So, cutting off his leg does a few things. It may or may not get us better information about Cole's whereabouts, but it will most certainly put the fear of man in this monster, if not the fear of God. It will also limit his ability to commit similar crimes.

"If you're gonna talk about mercy, you have to consider it for all those involved. Would it be merciful to society at large for us to put this depraved criminal back on the street without any consequences?

"Even if you think the answer is yes, would it be merciful to the criminal? Because he'll think the apocalypse is a license to pillage, rape, and steal with impunity. And if he pulls something like this again, odds are, the next group of survivors will put him down.

"Please don't think I enjoy this, but to me, this is the most loving, merciful thing I know to do. Considering all goes well, I'll present the man with the gospel, put fresh bandages on his leg, give him some antibiotics which your father had the forethought to stockpile, and send him on his way."

"I doubt he'll listen if it's coming from the man who cut his leg off."

"That will be between him and God. My hands will be clean. He's the one who chose this path."

Shane bargained, "Why not cut off his hand?"

"You only need one hand to pull the trigger."

"Sure, but couldn't the same be said about one leg?"

"Yes, but with one leg, he'd have a devil of a time navigating through all those brambles in the woods to get to us. Assuming he turns out to be the vindictive sort, that is."

Shane sighed with a heavy heart. "Cutting off the man's leg in this environment is a death sentence."

"You don't know that," replied Pastor Joel. "He

might have folks praying for God to bring him home by any means necessary. I know I've heard your parents pray a similar prayer. Remember what Jesus said. It's better to enter life maimed than to be cast into hell with all your hands and feet."

Shane wasn't sure about the pastor's reasoning, but he certainly didn't have the same level of conviction concerning letting the man keep his leg as he'd had only minutes ago.

"Are you good with this?" Pastor Joel asked.

Shane thought a while longer. "I don't know."

"If you want to put it to a vote, you're welcome to it. But if we don't do it my way, you'll have to bear the burden of either setting the man free without consequences or putting a bullet in his head once everything is said and done."

Shane took a deep breath and opened the door. "We'll do it your way."

Shane watched as Pastor Joel cut away the duct tape on the man's feet with a pair of EMT shears. Next, he used the shears to remove the man's pant leg. He then cleaned the area he'll be cutting with betadine from the medical kit."

"What are you doing?" the hostage cried.

"I'm gonna peel back the flesh for you. If I start with the bone saw straight into the skin, it's going to make a real mess of things. This will allow you to heal up much quicker. You'll thank me later."

"Who are you people?"

"We're the folks who love that little boy you took. We're the folks who offered to give you a nice big diamond to bring him back. No questions asked." Pastor Joel tightened a tourniquet above the man's knee. "But now, we have to do things the hard way."

"Please! No!"

"Hold him steady," Pastor Joel instructed.

Shane grabbed his shoulders while Paul held his legs.

"The boy is in a trailer down by the river in Cullowhee."

"Good. Let's try to keep our answers specific."

The man's eyes were opened wide. "If I tell you, I get to keep my leg?"

"Nope. That's a done deal. You lost that when you double-crossed us down by the river. Now we're negotiating for your remaining three limbs." Pastor Joel cleaned the filleting knife from the skinning kit with alcohol. He began to make an incision just below the knee.

The man screeched in pain and terror. Shane held his shoulders and looked away from the gruesome scene, yet he felt as if the torture were carrying through to his own body. Shane breathed heavily. He wondered what type of sadistic madman Pastor Joel had been before his conversion.

Pastor Joel kept cutting and the man continued to scream.

"Let's take a little break," said Pastor Joel. He clamped off the blood vessels with hemostats, then tightly tied lengths of sterile suture around each one to stem the bleeding, "Where in Cullowhee is the trailer?"

The man panted for breath, seeming to enjoy his hiatus of suffering. "It's a trailer park. Old Cullowhee Road. Right before you get to the bridge that takes you to the university."

"Alright. Which trailer?"

"The boy is in the last one."

"How many people are guarding him?"

"Two men and two women are in that trailer."

"Any other children around?"

"No."

"You said that trailer. Are there more people from your group in the trailer park?"

"Please, if I tell you, you'll stop cutting?"

"I can't do that. But you can save yourself a lot of pain. For every one of our people who gets hurt on this mission, I'm taking off another limb when we get back." Pastor Joel shook the bottle of antibiotics. "And I'm taking these with me. If I don't come back, I guess you'll die of sepsis. That's a bad way to go."

The expression on the man's face showed that he regretted most every decision he'd made in life. As if in one way or another, they'd all led him down a path which had brought him to Pastor Joel's bloody confessional. "We have the back three trailers. The park only has about seven trailers total."

"Good. How many people are there?"

"Was twelve. Eight guys, four girls. But Jeff is dead, and I'm here, so ten."

"Six guys, four girls." Pastor Joel nodded and took out the bone saw.

The man pleaded and bucked, howled with blood-curdling shrieks. Shane used all his might to keep the man's shoulders pinned to the plywood table while Pastor Joel sawed at the bone. It seemed to Shane an eternity. He could only imagine how elongated the torment must be for the man. But then again, he could not even fathom the dread which poor little Cole Stanley must be going through.

The man's wails grew weaker. Shane heard a thump against the filthy pea gravel on the musty floor of the basement. He looked to see the bloody leg. His stomach turned. He felt dizzy and looked away quickly.

"Let's get you stitched up."

The hostage was still, breathing like a man who'd just run a marathon.

Fifteen minutes later, Shane glanced back at what Pastor Joel was doing. He was tying off the sutures.

"I guess that's it," said Pastor Joel.

"We need to get going. I've got a map at the main cabin. We have to put together an attack plan." Paul's voice showed the displeasure in what he'd just taken part. However, he'd never voiced his objection, as if, like Pastor Joel, he saw it as a necessary evil.

"I need to wash up real quick," said Pastor Joel. "We can lock the door. His hands are still secure. I don't think he'll go anywhere. Especially if he knows what's good for him. Rolling around on this floor with that wound will definitely get him a life-threatening infection."

Paul seemed to have trouble looking Shane in the eye. "Son, will you go rally the rest of the men? This is going to require all of us. Your mom and sister can shoot, so can Maggie Farris and the pastor's wife. The women can hold down the fort while we're gone."

"Julianna can shoot also," Shane added.

Paul glanced at the feeble, butchered being on the make-shift table. "For his sake, it might be best if we keep guns away from Julianna for a while."

"Should someone guard the gate?" Shane headed for the door.

"I'll put Angela on the entrance while we're gone. Kari Ensley, too, I'm sure she can shoot."

Shane nodded on his way out the door to gather Greg, Dan, and Fulton.

CHAPTER 23

Have not I commanded thee? Be strong and of a good courage; be not afraid, neither be thou dismayed: for the Lord thy God is with thee whithersoever thou goest.

Joshua 1:9

The men from the compound geared up and gathered in the basement guest room of the main cabin. Normally, this room was Bobby's bedroom, but he seemed not to mind that it had been temporarily converted into a war planning room.

Using his phone, Shane pulled up the satellite image of the area on the map which his father pointed to. "We could split into two teams. One team can continue over the bridge and circle around to Ledbetter. The river looks shallow enough to cross in rubber mud boots."

Paul took Shane's phone and examined the proposed routes. "I think that could work. The problem will be watching out for crossfire. If the front team is shooting, they'll have to remember that the rear attack force has only paper-thin trailer walls to protect them from stray bullets. I don't have to remind any of you that a trailer wall is little more than heavy-duty cardboard with a sheet of aluminum foil over top. It might stop a BB. Pellet guns and higher, I wouldn't count on it."

Will added, "My son is in the back trailer anyway. So over-penetration is already of paramount concern."

"Good point. Everyone, keep all of that in mind when you pull the trigger. We don't have time to practice this raid. If your mags aren't loaded with hollow points, see me to change out your bullets. If you hit your target with a hollow point, you shouldn't have to worry about the bullet traveling any further. If you're not sure of your shot, make sure the bullet is going to continue in a trajectory that will take it over your teammates' heads or under their feet. But, always be sure of your shot. With all that said, bringing Cole home is our priority. Do what you have to do.

"Bobby and Will, go with Shane. Son, you'll lead your team. The rest of us will come in the front of the trailer park. We'll hit first so Shane's team can use our gunfire as a distraction to slip in and rescue Cole."

"What about the women?" Bobby inquired.

"They're kidnappers. They should have known what they were signing up for." Paul's face showed his regret at the prospect of shooting a woman, but he obviously wasn't about to let it stand in the way of bringing Cole back to his mother.

Paul appeared to hesitate, but asked Pastor Joel, "Will you pray for us before we roll out?"

Pastor Joel seemed unsure if he were qualified after the dastardly thing he'd done to the hostage. Even so, he bowed his head. "Father, watch over us. Keep us safe on this mission. Bring Cole home." He paused. "Forgive us when we fall short. And grant us the wisdom to do what's right. Amen."

"Good prayer." Paul looked up. "See me if you need hollow point ammo. I'll give it to you and you can reload your magazines on the trip over. Let's roll out."

***

Shane's truck was operational, but he didn't feel comfortable relying on it after the collision with the van. Plus, the deflated airbag was still dangling from the steering wheel. Will volunteered to drive his truck. Shane's team followed Paul and Pastor Joel who would pull over and wait for Shane to tell them when they were ready to cross the river.

The small convoy raced south to Cullowhee. Paul called over the radio, "That's it, up ahead on the right. We'll stop here. Let us know when you're in position."

"Roger." Shane tried to get a look of the area while Will drove past, but it was down an embankment and hidden from view.

Will continued across the bridge and back up Ledbetter where he pulled off the shoulder of the road. "This is our spot."

Shane looked at Bobby's feet. "You're wearing those boots? You'll freeze."

"Nobody had any rubber boots that would fit me. I put trash bags under my socks to keep my feet dry. I'll be alright. I've got dry socks and sneakers to put on after the smoke clears."

Shane wished the big man were better equipped but appreciated his sense of duty. "We'll cross the river here. It looks shallow enough. Stay low and keep that thicket of shrubs between us and the trailers."

Shane stepped into the icy water. Instantly, he felt the heat leave the inside of his boot. He turned back to Bobby as he entered the river. "You alright?"

"It's chilly, but I'll make it."

Shane put his arm out to keep Will from passing him. "Take it easy. We'll get Cole." He understood that Will was anxious to get his son back, but rushing a delicate situation like this could cause more harm than good.

Once they'd forded the river, Shane signaled for them to hunch down behind the trees. He reduced the volume and whispered into the radio. "We're in position."

"Good. Make your way up to the trailer. Have Bobby peek in the windows and see if he can get eyes on Cole. We'll launch our attack in two minutes." Paul's transmission ended.

Shane motioned for them to follow as he worked through the brush to the back side of the trailer. When they drew closer, Shane placed a hand on Will's shoulder, indicating for him to stay put. He motioned for Bobby to approach the windows and look inside.

Bobby reconnoitered the dwelling and stealthily returned to the shrubs. He pointed to the corner of the trailer closest to the river. "The little boy is lying on a mattress near the outside wall. One woman is in a chair by the door, watching TV. She has a shotgun. The other corner of the trailer is the kitchen. From there, I could see into the living room. That's where everyone else seems to be gathered. I counted two other women and two men, but I couldn't see around the wall. They're ready for trouble. I guess they figured when the other two men didn't come back that a rescue attempt was bound to happen."

"Think you can hit the woman in the chair through the window with your pistol?" Shane asked.

"No problem," Bobby said with confidence.

Will shook his head. "That will frighten Cole to death."

Shane felt bad for his old friend from a bygone life. "I know, but she's likely to use him as a human shield otherwise."

"Or she could have orders to kill him if they're attacked." Bobby's voice was sympathetic.

"We don't have any other choice." Shane pressed the butt of his AR-15 into his shoulder. "And Cole is probably already as scared as he can be."

Will nodded reluctantly. "Okay."

Shane patted him on the back. "When the other team begins the assault, you shoot the lock off the back door. I'll kick it in and press toward the living room eliminating anyone I see. You follow behind and mop up. They're expecting Dad's team to come in the front door. Hopefully, they'll never see us coming.

"Bobby, take out your target, then come on around and help us clear the rest of the rooms. Once we get Cole, Will can take him to the riverbank and keep him safe while Bobby and I go help Dad with any remaining hostiles."

Bobby nodded and slipped up toward the window. Will crouched low with his AR-15 ready to fire.

POP, POP, POP! The first sounds of gunfire echoed from three trailers away. Shane stepped to the side and allowed Will to blast the doorknob and deadbolt. Next, he kicked the door open and started shooting. He dropped one woman and one man before any of the others realized he was in the room. He advanced further inside to provide Will with room to come in and help. The two of them exchanged shots with the remaining woman and man at point blank range. Bobby soon arrived to back them up. Several more rounds were fired and the two other hostiles fell to the floor. Shane quickly put another round into each of the heads of the enemy casualties. "Let's clear the bathroom and the bedroom on the left before we go to Cole." He turned to see Will with his hand on his chest. His shirt was soaked with blood.

Will took a step as if determined to help clear the

trailer but then toppled to the ground. Bobby caught him from behind and eased his head against the wall.

Will forced a grin. "Maybe I'll just hang out here and make sure no one comes through the front door."

Shane knelt to get a better look at the wound.

Will shook his head. "Worry about me later. Just finish your job and get Cole out of here."

Shane tried not to let his concern show. "We'll get you fixed up in no time." He motioned for Bobby to follow him. They checked the bathroom, then the bedroom across the hall from Cole. Once they knew the trailer was secure, Shane opened the door to a terrified, crying little boy. "Cole, hey, I'm here with your dad. We're gonna take you home."

The little boy shrunk back into the corner, as if unsure about whether to trust Shane.

Shane knelt beside the mattress. "Let's go see your mama."

The boy whimpered. "Mama's here?"

"She's at the farm. But your dad's here." Shane pushed his rifle behind his back and held out his hand.

The boy took it and Shane led him out into the living room.

"Daddy? What happened?"

"Oh, it's just a scratch." Will's breath was labored. "Are you okay? Did they hurt you?"

"They gave me medicine that made me sleepy." The boy ignored the blood and latched on to Will.

"It'll wear off. You'll be fine." Will stroked Cole's hair, holding him close for comfort and assurance.

Gunfire continued in the next trailer over. Shane pressed the talk key of his walkie talkie. "We've got Cole. Will was hit. The trailer is clear. Do you need Bobby and me to come up there and lend a hand?"

Seconds later, Paul replied, "What's your count on dead hostiles?"

"Five," said Shane.

"We've got four. If our Intel was right, that means we've still got a floater around here somewhere. Keep your team there. Hold down the fort and guard Cole. We'll hunt down the last one."

"Roger." As soon as Shane had taken his finger off the talk key his imagination took over. All he could think about was the remaining thug catching his father off guard and shooting him from behind. "Bobby, you stay with Cole and Will. I'll be back."

Shane slipped out the front door and closed it quietly behind him. He lay prone on the ground and looked through the lattice for anyone on the other side of the trailer.

"Help! Help me, please!" cried a woman's voice.

"Take it easy." Pastor Joel's voice followed.

"These people, they were holding me hostage. I managed to get away when the shooting started. You have to help me get out of here."

"We'll help you. But keep your hands where we can see them." Paul's voice could be heard from the opposite side of the trailer.

"I think they're holding a little boy in the next trailer. They asked my family for ransom money. They're trying to get it together, but I don't know if they were going to let me go or not."

"Ma'am, we have to insist that you keep your hands where we can see them." Pastor Joel reiterated Paul's request.

Shane peered around the side to see the woman had a pistol tucked in the back of her jeans where none of the others could see it.

Oblivious to Shane's presence, she continued the charade. "I haven't eaten in like two days. Do you have any water? And maybe a phone so I can call my family?"

"She can use my phone," said Fulton.

"Thank you so much!" The woman put her hands on her hips, inches away from the pistol in her jeans.

"Let's pat her down first," said Greg.

"She's been through enough," countered Dan.

Shane raised his rifle as he watched her hand creep closer to the handle of the pistol.

Fulton came into view, his hand outstretched with the phone, and his rifle dangling out of reach behind him.

The woman looked ready to pounce. Shane guessed she intended to grab Fulton, and with a gun to his head, use him as leverage to escape. "Not on my watch," he whispered.

"I can't tell you how happy I am to see you!" She stepped forward and reached back.

"Fulton, watch out!" Paul called.

She put her hand on the gun. POW! Shane's rifle kicked back and the woman dropped to the ground.

"What did you do that for?" Greg asked.

Shane pointed at the pistol lying in the grass near her head. "She had a gun. She wasn't a hostage. She was our tenth combatant." He turned toward the far trailer. "Bring a truck to the rear trailer. We have to get Will to a hospital. He's been shot."

CHAPTER 24

But I would not have you to be ignorant, brethren, concerning them which are asleep, that ye sorrow not, even as others which have no hope. For if we believe that Jesus died and rose again, even so them also which sleep in Jesus will God bring with him.

1 Thessalonians 4:13-14

Shane pulled Cole away from his father.
"Daddy!" the boy cried.
"It's okay, Son," Will said with a feeble voice. "You go with Pastor Joel. He's going to take you to mama. I love you, Son."
"I love you, too, daddy," the boy sobbed. "Why can't you come?"
"I've gotta go to the doctor first. I'll see you

soon."

Cole seemed unsure of Will's claim but went with the pastor anyway.

Paul pointed to Greg, Dan, and Fulton. "Y'all ride back with Pastor Joel. We'll be along later."

On his way out, Pastor Joel said, "I'd take Will to Cliff Johnson instead of the hospital."

"The veterinarian?" Shane was surprised at the recommendation.

The pastor nodded. "The hospital has been short-staffed since all this started. Workers quit showing up when they stopped getting paid. Even most of the folks who do it out of love couldn't afford to keep going in with gas at $100 a gallon."

"Yeah, but a gunshot wound is going to be a priority," Shane argued. "If they're open at all, they'll treat Will first."

The pastor looked at Will. "Not if they think their efforts are in vain." He ushered the little boy out the door.

Shane grimaced. He and Bobby attempted to pick Will up to carry him from the trailer to the back seat of Paul's Ram.

Will moaned in agony. "Shane, please. I don't want to do this."

"We'll be as gentle as we can," Shane assured him.

"I'm not going to make it."

"You don't know that," Shane argued.

"Yes." Will's breaths were short. "I do."

Shane did not want to torture Will by moving him if it truly was no use. "Okay."

Will looked up at Bobby and Paul. "Can Shane

and I have a moment?" His voice was barely above a whisper. He struggled for each breath.

Paul nodded with a doleful face. He put his hand on Bobby. "We'll be out front. Call us if you need us."

Will closed his eyes, his breathing became more strained. "I loved Julianna." He took two more arduous breaths. His forehead creased heavily. "Long before you ever left." He opened his eyes to look at Shane. "But I never would have interfered." He closed his eyes once more. "Our friendship was far too important to me. I wanted you to know that."

Shane bit his lip and turned away. "I don't blame you. I thought Julianna would always be there. I thought I could go to Nashville, see how I liked the celebrity life, and if things didn't work out, I could go back to her. She deserved better than that.

"You two were close. It was a natural thing. I'm sorry that I let the jealousy and bitterness ruin our friendship."

Will's eyelids opened slightly. "I forgive you. I'm glad we had a chance to reconcile our differences."

Shane took the dying man's hand. "Me, too."

Will gripped Shane's hand firmly. "Look after her for me."

"Of course."

"Even if she doesn't want you to."

Shane's smile was bittersweet. "Even if she doesn't want me to."

Tears trickled down Will's cheek. "Take care of Cole. Teach him to be a man. Teach him to love God."

Shane lowered his body to the floor to embrace his old friend. How he wished they'd put aside their differences sooner. "I will, I promise. I won't let you down again." Shane ran his sleeve across his own eyes to dry them.

"I know you won't. Tell Juliana I love her. And make sure you have that talk with her." Will opened his eyes one last time. "I'll see you on the other side."

Shane watched him exhale softly, not to draw another breath.

***

Tonya Black met Shane, Paul, and Bobby at the backdoor of the main cabin. "Shhhh. Cole is sleeping off whatever they gave him."

"How is he?" Shane asked quietly.

Tonya hugged her son. "Doped up. But Julianna gave him a quick bath, got some food in his belly, and is letting him sleep on the couch with his head in her lap."

Shane walked into the living room. He watched the tenderness between mother and child while Julianna gently stroked Cole's hair. Her eyes were fixed on the child, gazing at him as if in a state of utter bliss. She looked up with loving eyes and a mellow smile. She whispered, "Where's Will?"

Shane swallowed hard. He turned his eyes away from hers, glancing at the boards of the deep, dark wooden floor. He should not be the one to convey the news. It should not come from him. Too many conflicts of interest. Too much emotion. A far too strained relationship. He looked back to his father, but Paul stood several feet behind him, tight-lipped, with no apparent intention of relieving Shane of this burden.

Shane turned his attention back to Julianna who had already lost her easy, pleasant expression. He knelt beside the resting child and watched her face contort into tormented woe. The task had been given to him. No one else would relay Will's final message. "He said to tell you he loves you."

She looked away from Shane, but he could still see the steady stream rushing down the left side of her delicate face. Shane took a tissue from the end table. He attempted to put it to her cheek. In a flash of viciousness, she struck his hand, knocking it away. She held up her hand like the claws of an injured jaguar, ready to strike again if he got too near.

Shane's chin sunk closer to his chest as he inched away from the grieving widow. His eyes turned to his mother. He got up from the floor, begging Tonya with his gaze for instruction on how to handle the situation.

"You can't help her, Son." Tonya embraced him. "You'll have to let her mourn. The Holy Spirit and time will have to do their thing. She's gonna need a lot of both."

***

Sunday morning's church service was canceled to make way for Will's funeral. A few of the people from Grace Chapel were in attendance. Will's grave was dug at a peaceful place down near the creek, only a few yards away from Lilith's. A simple wooden cross at the head of a mound of red dirt was all that marked Will's final resting spot.

Tonya walked Cole to the house to get him something to eat. Pastor Joel urged the others to offer their condolences and leave Julianna to grieve in peace. The nearby neighbors from church and other residents of the compound trickled away, one by one until only Julianna and Shane remained. Julianna sat on a simple bench Shane had constructed by splitting a six-foot length of a pine log. He'd notched it out at both ends to keep it from rolling and placed shorter sections of the log beneath to prop it up off the ground.

Shane leaned against a large hickory tree near the babbling brook. With all his heart, he wanted to give Julianna the time he knew she needed. Yet he remembered Will's final prompting to have a talk with her. Speculating on what he could learn from such a conversation nagged at him, making him restless in mind and spirit. Shane slowly walked over to the bench, not daring to sit beside her.

To his surprise, Julianna was the one to break the jagged silence between them. She did not look at Shane, but asked, "What will you do with the hostage who gave you the information about Cole's location?"

"Pastor Joel wants to take him back to the trailers."

"When will you do that?"

"Tomorrow afternoon."

"He isn't dangerous?"

"He's only got one leg, so I'm not sure he'll even be able to survive. We searched all three trailers, which his gang was using as a compound. We took all the guns and ammo. We left the corpses. I can't imagine he'll stay there. The smell will be intolerable. My guess is that he'll gather whatever he can carry and hobble off to find someone to take him in."

She said nothing, neither approving nor denouncing Pastor Joel's recommendations.

Shane steeled himself for the next route of the dialogue. "Will and I had a chance to reconcile our differences before . . ." Shane didn't know what word to use.

"That's good," she said with little enthusiasm.

"Will also said I needed to have a talk with you."

"Oh?" She crossed her arms and turned slightly on the bench so that her back shielded her perfectly from Shane. "About what?"

"He didn't say." Shane felt awful. "He seemed to think you'd know."

She was silent for a long while. Julianna turned slightly as if to check that Shane was still present. "After you left to go to Nashville . . ." A long sigh preceded her next words. "I found out I was pregnant."

Shane tried to keep the conversation moving. "Before you and Will got married?"

"Yes."

"I see." In the spirit of reconciliation, Shane tried to be graceful with his accusation. "When I heard that you two had gotten married so quickly, I kind of guessed that something must have been going on between you and Will while we were still together."

"Yeah, right!" She shook her head and scoffed, as if Shane were the dimmest of idiots.

"Am I missing something?"

"Will and I never even slept in the same bed until months after Cole was born."

"What? I don't understand."

"That night, before you left. I thought I could change your mind. I thought that was why you were leaving because I wouldn't sleep with you. I thought maybe you'd stay or at least offer to take me with you. I was so stupid."

In a microsecond, all the implications of what Julianna was saying hit him like the side of a mountain. Shane felt dizzy. The ground beneath his feet wobbled and shifted. The sun darkened from his periphery inward until everything went black.

Shane awoke, as if from a deep sleep. He opened his eyes to the leaves and twigs in the forest floor. The sound of trickling water soon reminded him where he was and how he'd gotten there. Shane looked up to see Julianna still sitting on the bench, her facing him just as before. He slowly stood up and brushed the debris off of his shirt and pants.

She'd obviously not so much as turned to see if he were still alive. "Now you know how I felt."

"But it was only one time!" Shane grappled with reality.

"How many times do you think it takes?"

Shane's brain raced to formulate a response. "Why didn't you tell me?"

"I left you three messages on your phone."

The guilt stabbed him in the center of his gut.

Her voice held the echo of rejection. "You never called back."

"But if I had known…"

"Then what? You'd have run back and married me out of a sense of duty? Wow! How romantic that would have been." She turned to him. She looked through piercing eyes like daggers, her face glowing crimson with anger. "You wouldn't answer your phone anyway. Did you expect me to go hunt you down in Nashville like a stalker?"

Awash in regret and self-loathing, Shane said, "I'm so sorry. I'd give anything to go back and do everything over."

"And that absolves you of all your sins, Shane Black." Once more, she gave him the back of her head. After another long bout of soundlessness, she said, "What's done is done. I should have done things differently, too.

"When you wouldn't return my calls, I poured out my heart to Will. I told him how frightened I was of raising a baby on my own. I told him how awful it would be for me at church, how everyone would look at me, how I'd probably be asked to resign from the worship team. I didn't want to have the rest of my life defined by one stupid mistake. Will offered to marry me. It solved a lot of those fears. But it created some new problems.

"In the end, I felt like everyone knew anyway. Only now, I'm a liar in addition to being a whore. Cole looks exactly like you. I can't believe you never even suspected it. I can tell your parents do; by the way they look at him."

Shane replied, "I told Will that I'd look after

you. He asked me to help raise Cole."

"Neither of those things are going to happen. So just forget about it right now." Her response was cool, but Shane sensed an underlying torrent just below the surface.

"I understand why you're angry with me. I let you down and I let Cole down. But it's not fair to Cole to keep him in the dark. Please don't punish him because of my mistake. I'm not suggesting that it be now, but sooner or later, you have to tell Cole the truth."

"I don't have to tell Cole anything!" She stood up from the bench. "Because you're not his father. You're just the sperm donor. Will is Cole's father. This changes nothing. Will was the one who was there when Cole was born. Will rocked him to sleep when he was teething. Will held his hand when he took his first step. It was Will who Cole was calling the first time he said dada. It was Will who gave his life to bring Cole home."

Tears streamed down Julianna's face which glowed blazing hot with fierce rage, as bright red as her flame-colored hair. "You never were anything to Cole, you are nothing to him now, and if I have anything to say about it, you'll never be anything to him! Do you understand me, Shane Black? You're nothing to my son, and you're less than that to me." She sobbed uncontrollably.

Despite the well-deserved verbal assault, Shane opened his arms to embrace her.

She glared at him through the tears. With her teeth set together like a growling lioness and snarled lips, she said, "Don't—even—think about it!"

"Can I at least walk you back to the house?"

"I've made it this long without you." She crossed her arms tightly and stomped up the hill. "I'm sure I can manage to get back to the cabin without your assistance."

Shane lowered his gaze and stepped back. Everything Will had said was true. Like King David, Shane had been so consumed by anger toward Julianna and Will, so certain of their guilt, he'd never considered that he might be the real criminal in the story.

CHAPTER 25

The most terrifying words in the English language are: I'm from the government and I'm here to help.

Ronald Reagan

After Julianna had left, Shane knelt by Will's grave. "I gave you my word. I'll look after them, even though she wants no part of it." He stood up, glanced at Lilith's grave, and ventured back across the narrow stream. Shane trudged up the hill toward the long gravel driveway which led back to the house. His radio suddenly came to life.

Bobby's voice came through the speaker. "We've got a car coming toward the gate. I could use some backup."

Shane sprinted up the hill to the gate. Pastor Joel

had a much easier time coming from the direction of the trailers as he was coming downhill. Shane pointed to the black Lincoln Navigator rolling to a stop at the gate. "Any idea who that could be?"

"Looks like my no-account brother's vehicle."

"Is he still the mayor?"

"As long as money can buy votes, he is. But that day may be coming to a close." Pastor Joel patted Shane on the back. "Come on, let's go see what he wants."

"Good afternoon, Mayor," said the pastor.

A robust balding man wearing a dark blue suit closed the door of the Navigator. "Howdy, Joel."

"What brings you all the way out here?" Pastor Joel put his foot on the bottom rung of the gate which stood like a monument of bitterness between two brothers.

Paul Black's white Ram crackled against the gravel, coming to a stop right behind Shane, Bobby, and Pastor Joel.

Paul exited the driver's side door. Greg came out of the passenger's side.

"Afternoon, Paul," said Mayor Hayes.

Shane's father offered a nod. "Mayor."

"My wife told me about Will Stanley. She heard from one of the ladies who used to attend Grace Chapel. I just stopped by to pay my respects."

"That was kind of you, Wallace. I'll pass your message along to the bereaved." Pastor Joel stepped back from the gate as if to dismiss himself and the others.

The mayor looked at Paul. "I drove all this way, using precious fuel. Aren't you at least going to invite me in?"

Paul caught the glance from Pastor Joel. "I apologize, Mayor Hayes. The services have already adjourned and the widow has had a rough day. We all have."

"Better than yesterday." Wallace Hayes leaned on the gate with both elbows. "I understand there was no police report filed for Will's death."

"We called 911 to report the kidnapping of Cole Stanley." Paul stepped closer to the metal barrier between them. "It seems they were short on resources and unable to help. We had no choice but to take matters into our own hands to bring him home. Besides, we're in the county. The place where Cole was being held was also in the county. It wouldn't fall under Sylva's jurisdiction."

He gave a saccharine smile. "I checked with the Jackson County Sheriff's Office. No report has been filed there either. You understand that Sheriff Hammer and I share common interests."

Pastor Joel held a stern expression. "I understand that he was elected the same way most other county officials came into office, by campaign contributions from your political action committee. If that's what you mean by common interests, then yes, we're all very well aware."

Wallace Hayes grinned at Paul. "What's the Good Book say? Something about brothers being born for adversity? To hear him tell it, everybody would think *I* was the one who'd done time in prison and that *he* was the one who'd dedicated his life to public service."

"Public service?" asked the pastor. "You've done

quite well for yourself. Jackson Construction has made a lot of money doing public service."

"Jackson Construction is a private company," said Mayor Hayes.

"Of which you hold a controlling interest. Seems most of the other share-holders have conspicuous ties to local government as well."

"I don't award the contracts for the city. And I certainly have no control over who gets the jobs in the county."

"Not you personally," countered Pastor Joel. "But you've made sure everyone who does, is tied to the purse strings of your political action committee."

"I'm not here to bicker." Mayor Hayes addressed Paul, "I thought I'd give you the courtesy of personally bringing out a copy of the new census while I was here." He removed an envelope from his pocket and passed it over the gate.

Paul looked at the envelope but did not take it. "A census? For what?"

"We want to keep track of where everyone is ending up. Lots of folks relocating, coming together to farm, form militias, or whatever. If we know where everyone is at, we'll be in a better position to help. The form simply asked for the names, social security numbers, and dates of birth for everyone living on your property." Mayor Hayes glanced at Greg, Shane, and Bobby. "Seems you've got a few other guests staying with you beside my cantankerous brother."

"From the response we got when we called about Cole's abduction, it doesn't seem you're in much of a position to help at all, Mayor Hayes." Paul took a step away from the envelope still pointed at him like a gun. "Since a census is voluntary, I'll exercise my right to decline."

"This is a mandatory census, Mr. Black." Hayes waved the envelope, holding his arm further across the top rail of the gate.

"Mandatory?" Paul's brow creased. "Seems the first record of a mandatory census I can remember hearing about was the one issued by Caesar at the birth of the Messiah. If I understood the story correctly, it was mandatory because it was tied to a tax. Is there some correlation here?"

Mayor Hayes cleared his throat. "Obviously, without adequate income or savings to pay property taxes, some residents may find themselves in foreclosure of tax liens. It's in everyone's best interest if we have some alternative method in place to collect revenues. We have full faith in the federal government and the new gold dollar to resolve our current fiscal crisis, but it never hurts to have a backup plan. According to the rumor mill, Paul, you've been a long-time proponent of that philosophy."

"My philosophies are my own, Mayor. I wouldn't believe everything you hear if I were you," Paul retorted. "Anyway, property taxes are a county issue."

"Once again, I'll remind you that the city and the county's interests are aligned."

"Then you tell the folks at the Jackson County Tax Collector's office to mail me my bill. If the mail quits running, tell them to send it by courier.

I'll make sure it gets paid the same as I always have." Paul turned away from the man. "Greg, you hang around with Bobby for a while to watch the gate until the next shift starts."

"Sure," said Greg.

"Pastor, Shane, let's get on back up to the house." Paul started walking to the truck. "Mayor, have a nice evening."

"We'll be seeing you again soon, Paul." The mayor's voice was just short of threatening.

Shane got in the back of the Ram and closed the door. "He's going to be trouble, isn't he?"

Pastor Joel closed the passenger's door when he entered the vehicle. "He always has been. Predators thrive in this type of environment. It doesn't matter which side of the law they happen to fall on."

Paul started the engine. "We need to get in front of this thing. I'll start talking to the folks on the neighboring farms tomorrow. We need a strong citizen response to nip this right in the bud before the mayor's scheme can take hold."

Once they'd finished the short ride up the steep driveway, Shane said, "Dad, can I speak to you for a moment?"

Paul nodded. "Pastor Joel, I'll talk to you later."

Shane watched the pastor enter the cabin and close the door.

"What's going on?" Paul seemed to know the topic of the conversation would be an important one.

Shane proceeded to tell his father about Cole and the situation with Julianna.

Paul put his hand on Shane's shoulder. "I don't

think anyone will be surprised about that. Especially your mother. The boy looks just like you. We'll do everything we can for Julianna. We always have. We genuinely love her and Cole, but our suspicions have prompted us to take more of an interest in their wellbeing than we might have otherwise."

"I can count on you to not say anything to anyone else besides Mom?"

Paul grinned. "I won't discuss it with anyone. I never have talked about it with anyone except your mother. But this one is on you. Part of being a man and accepting responsibility is facing the music with your mom. You need to be the one who tells her."

Shane hated the thought of how she'd look at him when he told her. He was ashamed that he'd missed out on being Cole's father, but it didn't end there. Cole, Julianna, and his entire family were bearing the brunt of his mistake. Yet, for some reason, depriving his mother of the opportunity to be Cole's grandma seemed the most dastardly of sins. His neck slumped as if he were trying to hide between his own shoulder blades. "Okay, I'll tell her."

***

The next morning, Shane closed the front gate behind his father, Fulton, and Dan. "Y'all be safe."

"We're just having some friendly conversations with the neighbors about this census business." Paul waved. "I doubt we'll get into any firefights."

Shane forced a smile, but he knew all too well

that trouble needed no invitation, especially since the crisis began. He turned to Pastor Joel who was on duty with him. "I hope he's right about that."

"The Lord will watch over them," replied the pastor.

Shane wanted to believe the statement to be true. However, he felt more skeptical about faith than the pastor did.

An hour later, his worst fears were realized. The silence was broken by a nearby gunshot.

"That came from the guest cabin." Pastor Joel said, but Shane was already running toward the sound.

Shane took out his radio as he sprinted to the small house where his sister lived. "Bobby! Gunshots at the guest cabin! Meet me there!"

"On my way," said Bobby over the walkie.

Shane slowed his step and approached from the concealment of the surrounding trees. He scanned the immediate area through the reflex sight of his AR-15. Seeing no one on the lawn or porch, he continued closer, working his way around the yard to the drive-up basement entrance on the far side.

Shane lowered his rifle when he saw the shooter, but kept running. "Julianna! Are you okay?"

She stood with a semi-automatic pistol in her hand, the large wooden swing door to the basement opened wide. "I won't have our son looking over his shoulder the rest of his life, wondering if that monster is going to come back. If you want to be part of his life, you need to step up. Get used to making tough decisions like this. It's the least you can do."

Pastor Joel arrived soon after Shane. "Julianna, what have you done?" He rushed into the open basement, kneeling next to the man leaking copious amounts of red fluid. The pastor examined the one-legged hostage, checking for a pulse. Finding none, the pastor walked back outside. He scowled at Julianna. "Give me the gun."

She hit the magazine ejection button and racked the slide to kick out the live round in the chamber. "You have your own standard for mercy, Pastor Joel. As a mother, so do I." She handed him the gun and the magazine.

"I was completely powerless to protect my little boy from those monsters. I can do nothing about the nightmares and the horrific memories he'll have for the rest of his life. But I can make sure he doesn't have to worry about this one coming back.

"People questioned your decision to cut the man's leg off. I hope you'll take that into consideration when you, Paul, and the others decide how I should be punished for this action. But whatever the cost, I did what I had to do for my little boy."

Bobby arrived in time to catch the end of the conversation. He said nothing but looked at Shane as if he empathized with what Julianna had done.

The pastor did not. "For starters, you'll be the one who digs the grave and buries him. I can't say that will be the end of your consequences. I'll have to speak with the others. For now, I've got to get back to guarding the gate."

Pastor Joel still wore the angry glower on his face. "Come on, Shane."

"I'll give her a hand. She can't move the body by herself. Bobby, can you fill in for me at the front gate?"

Bobby gave a kind smile to Shane and Julianna. "Sure thing." He followed the pastor up the gravel drive.

Shane waited for them to be out of earshot. "So you changed your mind? You're going to tell Cole?"

"Give him some time to grieve over Will. I'll talk to him when the time is right. I guess it will have to be a birds-and-the-bees discussion as well. He's too young for all that, but thanks to you, I suppose we'll have to step up the timeline on that awkward moment." She took a shovel from the corner near the door.

Her neck snapped around toward Shane. She glared at him with warning eyes. "And if you have even the slimmest notion that you and I are going to raise him together, play house and all of that, you can wipe it out of your mind right now. It will never happen. Never, Shane Black!"

"I understand. Thanks for reconsidering; about Cole, I mean." Shane picked up another shovel, slung his rifle around his back and led the way toward the creek.

She followed him and her hostility softened. "Just don't hurt Cole. If you're planning on walking away again, he'd be better off if he never knew."

Though he remained guilt-ridden, Shane felt better about being able to keep his commitment to Will. But if he planned to teach Cole how to be a man, he needed to make some changes in himself first. Once made, he'd have to prove to God, Cole, Julianna, his parents, and himself that his transformation was permanent. Such a monumental task could only be achieved with time and resolution.

DON'T PANIC!

Inevitably, books like this will wake folks up to the need to be prepared, or cause those of us who are already prepared to take inventory of our preparations. New preppers can find the task of getting prepared for an economic collapse, EMP, or societal breakdown to be a source of great anxiety. It shouldn't be. By following an organized plan and setting a goal of getting a little more prepared each day, you can do it.

I always try to include a few prepper tips in my novels, but they're fiction and not a comprehensive plan to get prepared. Now that you're motivated to start prepping, the last thing I want to do is leave you frustrated, not knowing what to do next. So I'd like to offer you a free PDF copy of *The Seven Step Survival Plan*.

For the new prepper, *The Seven Step Survival Plan* provides a blueprint that prioritizes the different aspects of preparedness and breaks them down into achievable goals. For seasoned preppers who often get overweight in one particular area of preparedness, *The Seven Step Survival Plan* provides basic guidelines to help keep their plan in balance, and ensures they're not missing any critical segments of a well-adjusted survival strategy.

To get your **FREE** copy of ***The Seven Step Survival Plan***, go to **PrepperRecon.com** and click the FREE PDF banner, just below the menu bar, at the top of the home page.

Thank you for reading *Black Swan, Book One: Dysphoria*

Reviews are the best way to help get the book noticed. If you liked the book, please take a moment to leave a review on Amazon and Goodreads.

I love hearing from readers! So whether it's to say you enjoyed the book, to point out a typo that we missed, or asked to be notified when new books are released, drop me a line.
prepperrecon@gmail.com

Stay tuned to **PrepperRecon.com** for the latest news about my upcoming books.

If you've enjoyed *Black Swan*, you'll love my end-times thriller series,
The Days of Noah

In an off-site CIA facility outside of Langley, rookie analyst Everett Carroll discovers he's not being told the whole truth. He's instructed to disregard troubling information uncovered by his research. Everett ignores his directive and keeps digging. What he finds goes against everything he's been taught to believe. Unfortunately, his curiosity doesn't escape the attention of his superiors, and it may cost him his life.

Meanwhile, Tennessee public school teacher, Noah Parker, like many in the United States, has been asleep at the wheel. During his complacency, the founding precepts of America have been systematically destroyed by a conspiracy that dates back hundreds of years.

Cassandra Parker, Noah's wife, has diligently followed end-times prophecy and the shifting tide against freedom in America. Noah has tried to avoid the subject, but when charges are filed against him for deviating from the approved curriculum in his school, he quickly understands the seriousness of the situation. The signs can no longer be ignored, and Noah is forced to prepare for the cataclysmic period of financial and political upheaval ahead.

Watch through the eyes of Noah Parker and Everett Carroll as the world descends into chaos, a global empire takes shape, ancient writings are fulfilled, and the last days fall upon the once-great United States of America.

If you have an affinity for the prophetic don't miss my EMP survival series, ***Seven Cows, Ugly and Gaunt***

In ***Book One: Behold Darkness and Sorrow***, Daniel Walker begins having prophetic dreams about the judgment coming upon America for rejecting God. Through one of his dreams, Daniel learns of an imminent threat of an EMP attack which will wipe out America's electric grid and most all computerized devices, sending the country into a technological dark age.

Living in a nation where all life-sustaining systems of support are completely dependent on electricity and computers, the odds of survival are dismal. Municipal water services, retail food distribution, police, fire, EMS and all emergency services will come to a screeching halt.

If they want to live, Daniel and his friends must focus on faith, wits, and preparation to be ready . . . before the lights go out.

You'll also enjoy my series about the coming civil war in America, *Ava's Crucible*

The deck is stacked against twenty-nine-year-old Ava. She's a fighter, but she's got trust issues and doesn't always make the best decisions. Her personal complications aren't without merit, but America is on the verge of a second civil war, and Ava must pull it together if she wants to survive.

The tentacles of the deep state have infiltrated every facet of American culture. The public education system, entertainment industry, and mainstream media have all been hijacked by a shadow government intent on fomenting a communist revolution in the United States. The antagonistic message of this agenda has poisoned the minds of America's youth who are convinced that capitalism and conservatism are responsible for all the ills of the world. Violent protest, widespread destruction, and politicians who insist on letting the disassociated vent their rage will bring America to her knees, threatening to decapitate the laws, principles, and values on which the country was founded. The revolution has been well-planned, but the socialists may have underestimated America's true patriots who refuse to give up without a fight.

ABOUT THE AUTHOR

Mark Goodwin holds a degree in accounting and monitors macroeconomic conditions to stay up-to-date with the ongoing global meltdown. He is an avid student of the Holy Bible and spends several hours every week devoted to the study of Scripture and the prophecies contained therein. The troubling trends in the moral, social, political, and financial landscapes have prompted Mark to conduct extensive research within the arena of preparedness. He weaves his knowledge of biblical prophecy, economics, politics, prepping, and survival into an action-packed tapestry of post-apocalyptic fiction. Having been a sinner saved by grace himself, the story of redemption is a prominent theme in all of Mark's writings.

"He brought me up also out of an horrible pit, out of the miry clay, and set my feet upon a rock, and established my goings." Psalm 40:2

Made in the
USA
Lexington, KY